I0452169

NOGGLE STONES

BOOK II: THE TRAGIC EMPIRE

Written and Illustrated by

Wil Radcliffe

Front and Back Covers by

Malcolm McClinton

Noggle Stones, Book II: The Tragic Empire

Published by R Corners Publishing

ISBN: 0615810357

R Corners Publishing
Coldwater, MI
USA

www.nogglestones.com

For Loubna

CHAPTER 1
A GOBLIN'S PERSPECTIVE

There were a great many words to describe how Bugbear felt about being chained upside-down in an Áes dána dungeon. Some of these words he had overheard at a particularly rowdy inn the other night during a particularly contentious game of cards. However, the goblin felt it best not to dwell on these words. It was very counter-productive to have such dirt polluting one's mind. Better to concentrate on the positive aspects of the situation. Such as the food, which tasted rather good for prison fare... despite the fact that most of it ended up caked in his nostrils and hair, due to the logistical difficulties of eating while chained upside-down in an Áes dána dungeon.

It was then, whilst Bugbear pondered his peculiar fate, that with a sudden slam, stomp, and huff, a guard entered the chamber. While his manner was rough and rude, his appearance, like most Áes dána, was pristine and impeccable... his cloak a blood red waterfall cascading down his back, his armor a rich silver tapestry of intricate etchings, and his helm a spired monument sprouting from his head like a stag's antlers. One could be both awed and repulsed when gazing upon such a beautiful and horrific creature, all the more so due to the slender, shimmering blade poised in his hand.

"You will answer questions now, goblin," the guard growled.

"Gladly," Bugbear said with a stifled yawn. "I'm itching for a good conversation. And seeing as how there are no rats and roaches in your tidy little dungeons, I'll settle for sharing syllables with an overly-adorned fop such as yourself."

The guard frowned and fumed. It almost seemed that his rage coupled with his over-sized helmet would send him teetering over like a tree struck by lightning. "Who do you serve?" he finally barked, after sifting through his bitter frustrations.

"Whom," Bugbear said.

"And this *Whom*, from what kingdom does he hail?"

Bugbear sighed. "No," he said with a shake of his head, which flaked off a crust of raspberry tart that had lodged in his mutton chops. "*Whom* is not a person. Rather it is the correct form of the pronoun you were attempting to use."

The guard looked to Bugbear, tilting his head with curiosity... before suddenly catching himself as the large helmet almost pulled him to the ground. "And this pronoun," the guard started, eyes narrow and hard as he attempted to regain his dignity, "how large are his armies?"

Bugbear laughed. "Oh, what delicious fare you Áes dána are! So paranoid and suspicious that you can only think in conspiracies and intrigue!" Bugbear let his laugh linger, trickling into a thin and whispering titter. "If you must know, I serve King Martin of the United Realm of Willow Prairie. I am on a vital fact-finding mission."

The guard stroked his chin, looking at Bugbear. "Then you are a spy," he said with a scowl.

"I am no more a spy than you are a scholar," Bugbear snorted. "I am searching for clues as to the identity of an ancient evil."

"Ancient evil?"

"Yes. So ancient that no living race seems to have any oral or written record of its existence."

"Faugh!" the guard laughed. "Impossible! The Áes dána Empire has existed since the dawn of time. Our records reach all the way back to King Oberon himself! The royal library is filled with records so ancient, the parchment they are written upon has petrified!"

"Oh, I find that hard to believe," Bugbear huffed. "Why everyone knows that the Coranieid Empire was far more ancient than the Áes dána. Their records were the most complete and thorough in all the world. Until their empire fell, of course, and their libraries were raided and burned."

"Ha!" the guard blurted. "Raided, yes. But only the buildings were burned. The Coranieid records remain intact to this day, safely held here in King Brenen's keep."

"Oh, really?" Bugbear said as his eyes narrowed in sly sarcasm. "Then it seems I was wise to let myself be captured."

"Let yourself?"

"Indeed!" Bugbear blurted as the chains fell from his body and he flipped heel over head to land gracefully on his feet. "For I am the razor edge of madness! And madness cannot be contained!"

The guard leveled his blade at Bugbear, trembling and weaving as he attempted to maintain his balance. "Stay where you are!"

"Certainly," Bugbear smiled. "But let me ask you something. Once a thought is thought, can it be stopped?"

"You speak nonsense!"

"Do I?" Bugbear said. "Or do I simply think it?"

The guard put his free hand up to his wobbling head, steadying his unwieldy helmet as well as his unwieldy mind. "Stop it."

"Stop a thought? I think not. Better to think it through. For only when it's thoroughly thought, will a thought think to stop."

The guard stumbled and fell against the wall, leaning his sword upon the ground.

"For example, I was thinking that perhaps somehow those chains behind you might suddenly snap about your arms and legs."

"Preposterous!" the guard sputtered.

Bugbear ached a brow. "Are you so certain? Chains and thoughts are related, are they not? Both can be linked. Both can be very heavy burdens. And both are your only company when held prisoner in an Áes dána dungeon."

The guard suddenly looked down to notice his hands and feet bound to the dungeon walls by thick and unyielding chains. "Witchcraft!" he blurted.

"No," Bugbear replied as he sauntered past on his way to the cell door. "Non-Logical Thought. There are four basic precepts of Non-Logical Thought, which can never be repeated enough. *Number one: Reality is Thought. Number two: Logic restricts Thought and thus restricts Reality. Number three: Abandon Logic, abandon restriction. And number four: Unrestricted Thought equals unrestricted Reality!*" Bugbear tapped the burdensome helmet so that it wobbled forward, teetered for a moment, then fell from the restrained guard's head. The guard blinked and looked about, as if suddenly seeing the world for the first time. "I have unrestricted your reality, young man. No thanks are necessary, however." The goblin then nodded to his erstwhile captor as he danced out the door.

As he scampered down the dark, yet strangely clean, hallways of the Áes dána keep, Bugbear let his head inflate with pride. His mastery of Non-Logical Thought was growing every day. More and more he was able to coax the unreal from the shadows of reality. Small miracles were at his fingertips. Delicate wonders were his to will. Minor marvels were at his command. Yes, ever since the Battle of Tamarack during which he and his apprentice, King Martin, temporarily merged into the dreaded Noggle Lord, his understanding of Non-Logical principles seemed limitless. Still, he realized caution was in order. There were legends that Whittlegrip, the renowned founder of Non-Logical Thought, had himself ventured too far into the unknown and thought himself into non-existence.

"Enjoying a stroll through our famous Halls of Hubris?" a haughty voice laughed, pulling Bugbear from his musings.

The goblin turned about to see a purple-robed Áes dána noble surrounded by several armed guards... with much smaller helmets and much larger swords than Bugbear's recent interrogator. They were quite human-like in appearance, apart from the most unnerving Áes dána trait of being nearly perfect and unblemished, and possessing an aura of stifling self-importance. In fact, it was said that members of Áes dána royalty must be perfect in both mind and body. Even the slightest scar prohibited a royal position. And many a mad monarch had been locked away in the castle tower to keep their rabid ravings from staining the royal reputation.

"The illustrious King Brenen, I presume," Bugbear said with an ingratiating smile and toadying bow.

"Ha!" King Brenen spat. "A goblin with courtly charm! Truly you are a miracle of nature!"

Bugbear laughed along with the nobleman. "Yes, I must confess, it is rare for my kind to show respect to Áes dána royalty. But understand. I represent not myself nor the goblin race, but good King Martin, who for some baffling reason insists that his envoys show respect to all peoples... whether they deserve it or not." Bugbear waddled up to the king, smiled a wide and bewildering smile, and shook the crumbs from his muttonchops and shirt collar right onto the king's rich purple cloak. "I truly enjoyed the food during my stay, by the way."

King Brenen looked down to the befouled garment, his face screwing up into a scowl, before suddenly relaxing into a smile.

"I have heard of you, Master Bugbear. I was eager to see how long it would take you to escape my dungeons. Going by the tales the wandering minstrels have spun, I would have thought your freedom quicker in the making... especially considering my best men have gone missing of late, and I had to make due with less qualified guards."

"Had I wished it, I would have never been taken prisoner in the first place," Bugbear said as he fell in beside the king for a leisurely walk down the hallway. "But you see, I had to be certain that you had what I hoped you had. Fortunately, one of your less discrete guards recently confirmed my suspicions."

"And what were those suspicions?" the king asked, looking down to Bugbear with an arched brow.

"That you were in possession of certain ancient Coranieid records."

"Hmmmm," King Brenen mused. "Yes. Then perhaps it was wise of you to remain in the dungeons where the tongues are loser and the heads are emptier. Had you escaped before discovering this, I most certainly would have denied being in possession of such scrolls. But, as you know, an Áes dána may lie only when it does not discredit another Áes dána. And so, as you have tricked the truth from one of my more fig-witted men, I admit to the charge."

"Excellent!" Bugbear piped. "Then you will show me to your library?"

"Certainly not!" the king laughed. "Simply because I admit that I own the records does not mean I shall allow you access to them!"

Bugbear sneered, glaring at the arrogant king with glittering, emerald eyes. Dark thoughts bubbled inside his head... and he wondered if his mastery of Non-Logic would allow him to transform flesh into raspberry jam. But that would most likely be considered an act of war, and King Martin would certainly frown upon that. Besides, he would never be able to find enough toast to make use of that much jam. Better to try a more diplomatic approach.

"King Brenen," Bugbear said, letting his face fall into an ingratiating grin. "Some months ago when King Martin invited various dignitaries and potentates to sign assorted treaties and alliances, your kingdom declined the invitation. Is this not true?"

"Yes," the king snorted. "We did not find it appropriate to offer aid, nor seek it from lesser folk. Although I understand the De Doty, Tuathian, and Dulwitch clans relented." Brenen turned up his nose as he spoke the names. "Danu's blood runs thin in their ranks, all the same."

"Yes," Bugbear sighed. "Pretenders and paupers, every last one of them. The dwarves and ogres too."

"Dwarves and ogres?" Brenen laughed. "Bah! To think an Áes dána would keep company with such rubbish!"

"Really," Bugbear laughed in agreement. "Even with the new railroad that will be connecting the allied kingdoms, it isn't worth being sullied with such associations!"

The king's laughter trailed into a pant. "Railroad?"

"Oh, yes!" Bugbear said. "The dwarves have been mining the sturdiest and purest iron for the project. And the ogres, they've been hauling lumber and laying tracks. And the humans, well their greatest inventors have been designing more powerful steam engines. Ten times faster than the swiftest Áes dána stallion, I'm told." Bugbear waddled from Brenen to gaze out a window into the courtyard. "Yes. With all of the new trade and commerce that will be sprouting up around your kingdom, you're much better off staying out of it. Wealth and success is so complicated, after all."

"The bards do not do you justice, Master Bugbear," the king sighed. "You are indeed the cleverest goblin since Twistroot. I submit to your superior deceit." And the nobleman offered a crisp, efficient bow to his goblin opponent. "Let us talk of treaties."

"It seems this day is filled with miracles," Bugbear chuckled. "A goblin with manners and an Áes dána with humility." Bugbear smiled as he pulled a parchment from his coat, walked to King Brenen, and held it up to him.

"You had a treaty already prepared?" the king said, looking to the goblin with suspicion.

"It's a standard treaty with a few spots left blank," Bugbear reassured. "So that the specifics can be filled in by the respective parties based upon the situation."

The king smiled as he looked over the parchment. "Seems a fair document. As for the specifics, I suggest that the Kingdom of Brenen shall provide safe passage for the alliance's railroad through our territories. In exchange, we ask for a chance to participate in free trade with the other kingdoms, and equal use of the railroad. Although, we request that we not be bound to any mutual defense obligations outside of our own borders."

"Understood," Bugbear said. "With one minor amendment... I require full access to your libraries."

King Brenen scowled. He stroked his chin. And he scoured the document. "Agreed. Let us..."

Something swift, loud, round, and metal entered the room. And it did not enter in a very courteous manner at all. It broke through the wall, bowled over the king's guards, and brought a peculiar, smoldering stink with it.

"Gun powder?" Bugbear coughed as he picked himself up. "A

cannonball?"

"We're under attack!" the king shouted. "To arms! Man the crossbows! Marshall the cavalry!"

Something swift, loud, round, and metal entered the room.

Soon gunfire peppered the air. Shouts, screams, and cries followed.

Bugbear waddled up to the mysterious missile that had ushered the chaos. As his hands and eyes wandered the surface, he came upon markings written in the human language of English.

"U.S. Army," he gasped.

CHAPTER 2
UNLEASHED

Somewhere in the night a child cried. It was a sound as sudden and cruel as a paper cut, as raw and terrifying as a flood of nightmares.

Manchester reined his horse to a stop in the town square. "Over here," he whispered to the shadowed riders behind him.

Maga and Mister Sagramore joined him, peering into the dark alleys.

"He's near," Maga said, as she struggled to keep her mount steady. "The horses can sense him."

"He might have a captive," Manchester said with a nod. "I heard a child..."

"Best to dismount," Maga said, swinging down from her saddle with little effort. "We'll have better luck catching him unawares without the horses. I'll take to the rooftops. You and Sagramore track him by the ground."

Manchester watched his queen sprint into the shadows and dart up a wall, her movements as startling and unnerving as her harsh demeanor. She had been his bride but a little over a year now, and every day he seemed to find some new difference between them... some trait to shake his faith, some quirk to stir his worries. He knew before he married her that she was more than human. But somehow, lately, Maga seemed less than human as well. More logical, less emotional. More calculating, less intuitive. More demanding, less giving. Manchester shuddered. It almost seemed that he married his demented goblin teacher, Bugbear, instead of the Maga he thought he knew.

"Your majesty," Sagramore said, breaking through the king's thoughts. "I believe the cry came just north of here, near the ruins of the old library."

"It figures that monster would hide in the ashes of knowledge," Manchester hissed as he stiffly lowered himself from his saddle.

"Waxing a bit poetic this evening, aren't we, your majesty?" Sagramore chuckled as he pulled a rifle from his saddlebag and fell in behind his king.

"I've told you before to forget all that 'majesty' nonsense, Sagramore," Manchester grumbled. "Call me Martin."

"The town of Willow Prairie has waited many years for the king promised in the prophecies," Sagramore said. "Now that you're here, it seems a shame to not be able to use the traditional titles."

"Use them at official functions if you must. But when we're alone, I'm simply a man."

"Martin," Sagramore snorted, "you defeated the Shadow Smith. There's very little that's simple about you."

Manchester considered responding, but he had discovered quite some time ago that there was little use in arguing against such admiration. The more he proclaimed his mediocrity, the more his subjects heaped praise upon him. In a sense, it was a perverse game of one-upmanship... an ironic contest in which the people proved his majesty by dismissing his opinions.

Besides, as Bugbear would no doubt point out had he been there, there was something useful about hero worship. He could call on any citizen at any time for any task. Even now a score of armed men and women circled the town to keep the beast from escaping into the forest.

The downside, of course, was that those men and women actually expected Manchester to confront and kill the threat. Killing was not something he relished. He much preferred the humanitarian aspects of kingship to the disciplinarian chores. Perhaps Maga would kill the pathetic creature before he even had a chance to draw his weapon.

Or perhaps the creature would kill him instead. Either way, he imagined his subjects would be disappointed in his performance.

No, Manchester abruptly thought. He shook the negative thoughts from his head as he followed Sagramore into the dark alley. If there was one thing he had learned under his apprenticeship with Bugbear, it was to deny failure. He would conquer the Barghest. He would subdue it. He would imprison it. His kingdom would remain safe.

They turned a corner and saw the terror. The Barghest hovered over a child... a girl, barely three years old. Saliva dripped from its boar tusks, pooling on the ground before the girl's feet. Feral eyes danced over the girl's limp form. Clawed hands opened and closed. Cloven feet stamped and pawed at the cobblestones. It was a nightmare... a twisted heap of deep, dark phobia summoned into reality.

"Leave the girl, Pawe," Manchester snarled, addressing the creature by the name it knew in its human life. The king leveled his pistol at the creature's head.

The patchwork creature turned to look upon his would-be captor. "Freedom," it growled.

"Never!" Maga screeched as she leapt from the rooftop, knocking the creature off its hooves and rolling with it to the alley wall.

"Hold your fire!" Manchester ordered, waving off Sagramore. The king lurched forward, holstering his gun for fear it might discharge and hurt Maga or the child. He quickly scooped the trembling girl into his arms, all the while eying his queen's life-and-death struggle with the beast. Rushing back to Sagramore, he handed off the child and turned his attention back to Maga and Pawe. Her blade had hit its mark several times... the monster was oozing blood from multiple wounds. But the Barghest had gotten a pawful of Maga's hair and was using it to unfair advantage, pulling her off balance. With the other claw it held down her sword arm. Manchester could see the creature readying its horns and fangs to finish off the helpless dragon bride.

Without hesitation Manchester drew the Bowie knife from the scabbard strapped to Sagramore's hip. "I need to borrow this," he hissed as he dove into the battle. He knew he was completely outmatched by the monstrous patchwork, but perhaps his training with Bugbear could give him some advantage. Perhaps if he imagined the Barghest already defeated, its head mounted on the wall over his fireplace, perhaps then he would find victory.

The horns slammed into Manchester, a mere graze, but powerful enough to knock him off his feet. The knife fell from the king's grasp and skittered across the cobblestones to the far end of the alley. So much for Non-Logic, Manchester thought. Perhaps he was better off relying on good old-fashioned human grit. Or a dose of good luck.

Manchester crawled to his feet, facing the beast, who had abandoned Maga in favor of more human prey. The Barghest snorted, its hot breath staining the cool night air. Manchester steadied his stance, hoping that some miracle would step between him and death.

A chorus of shouts broke the tension. The Barghest looked off in the direction of the commotion, as Sagramore took a shot with his buffalo rifle, driving a slug into the beast's shoulder. The patchwork let out an awful bellow before it charged Manchester. The king dropped to the ground and the beast leapt over him, thundering off into the night. Sagramore followed with a few more shots, but in its hunger for freedom, the Barghest was too fast.

Manchester helped Maga to her feet.

"I failed," she grunted, trying to hide the extent of her wounds.

"He was too much animal for the three of us," Manchester said. "Perhaps when Loomis and his brothers return tomorrow morning..."

"We cannot leave the defense of the kingdom in the hands of others!" the queen cursed. "I am your queen and your Chief Justice. Tonight I failed you."

"I failed as well," Manchester said, letting his hand fall into hers. "If not for the shouts of the crowd..."

It was then that Manchester turned his attention back to the flurry of shouting and cursing that was swiftly approaching them. Sagramore herded the girl towards the king and queen, taking up a defensive stance in front of them, his rifle at the ready. Manchester drew his pistol and Maga her sword.

A mob came into view... several townsfolk pushing and shoving a dozen or so well-dressed strangers. Manchester recognized the quality of the clothing and the regal bearing of those wearing it. They were Áes dána dignitaries... from Brenen's clan by the looks of their emblems.

"What's this?" Manchester demanded. "Why aren't you patrolling the forests outside of town?"

"These 'men,'" one of the townsfolk spat, "accosted us, demanding to see you!"

"We demand asylum in your kingdom," one of the Áes dána said, boldly stepping forward.

"We have no treaties with the Kingdom of Brenen," Manchester said. "Why would you seek asylum in Willow Prairie?"

"Because our kingdom has been attacked," one of the others added. "Our treasuries have been raided. Our king captured. Our sovereignty violated."

"By humans," another nobleman said as he spat on the ground.

"Humans?" Manchester said. "Impossible. All of my people have been busy with... internal affairs."

"It wasn't anyone from your kingdom, King Martin," the nobleman replied. "These were better trained humans. Warriors born. Brutal and unrelenting. And if that isn't enough to involve your kingdom in our dilemma, perhaps the fact that they've captured your pet goblin will stir your ire."

"Bugbear!" Manchester gasped.

"Martin," Maga said, placing a comforting hand on her king's shoulder. "We'll rescue him, I promise."

"And while we do that, who deals with the Barghest?" Manchester said with a weary shake of his head. "Get these men some food and find them quarters for the night. Mother Twitchett's boarding house will do."

The makeshift militia marched Willow Prairie's newest tourists onto the streets, leaving Manchester and Maga alone in the alley.

"Perhaps I can call upon my sisters," Maga suggested.

"Yes," Manchester agreed. "Send word. Have them rescue Bugbear. But tell them not to engage the human troops in battle. I want to know who they are and what they want before we stir things up any more."

"A sensible decision. I shall send out a messenger tonight. Then with the dragon brides looking into the attack on Brenen, that will leave us free to pursue the Barghest."

Manchester had to suppress a laugh that suddenly tried to lunge through his lips. An ethical man could never be *free*. That he realized. He would always be obligated to friends, family, country, God. Manchester looked to Maga, her eyes still wet with rage, her face flush with frustration. Wife.

The night air carried the triumphant cry of the Barghest. The forest would tremble tonight. The animals would cower. The trees would splinter. The night would be drenched in dread.

The Barghest... he had freedom.

CHAPTER 3
THEY CALL HIM ASHERBY

The smoke stung Bugbear's nostrils, teasing his tearing eyes open and forcing his sour mouth into a yawn. He blinked several times before inching up into a sitting position. His weary head turned, letting his weary eyes wander over his surroundings. He sat in the middle of a camp, exposed to the elements with only a tattered blanket to protect him from the autumn chill. Behind him huddled a few dozen Áes dána prisoners, tattered, battered and chained. Before him human soldiers hustled to and fro in the early morning hours, hauling ammunition and supplies, and barking orders like rabid dogs. Then there was the smoke, rising from a bonfire like souls reaching for Heaven. The soldiers heaped fuel onto the fire, and as Bugbear's tired eyes focused, he could see the exact nature of this fuel.

"Books!" Bugbear screamed. "No!" He lunged forward, intent on putting a halt to the tragedy, but something tugged him back to the ground. Chains. Once again some intellectual insect sought to hold him through such mundane means. With a shrug and a thought he attempted to shed the bonds, but as he walked forward again, the chains once more pulled him back. "Impossible!" he gasped.

"Not really," said an approaching tall man.

Bugbear quickly looked over this stranger in his fine black clothing. The goblin imagined he was an undertaker, lawyer, or some other breed of vulture in human guise. "What is the meaning of this?" Bugbear spat.

The tall man removed a small vial from his vest, examining it in the morning light. "This is the meaning," he said. "A potion, made from a new plant our scientists recently discovered. You goblin-folk have known about it for a while now. I believe you call it banderberry root."

Bugbear gasped and shuddered.

"We injected you with it after we found you unconscious in the ruins of Brenen's keep." The tall man placed the vial back into his vest pocket. "We mere humans haven't had many dealings with you fey folk. But we do know that goblins and Áes dána aren't likely to keep company. That is unless the goblin happens to be the famous Bugbear, renowned advisor to King Martin of Willow Prairie." The tall man held up the unsigned treaty Bugbear had presented to Brenen the day before. "Shouldn't leave official documents with your name on them laying about."

"But how did you know about banderberry root?" Bugbear asked.

"I said we haven't had much experience with fey folk, not that we were completely ignorant. We've captured and interrogated a few goblins here and there. Many of them were already addicted to the stuff. Others were quite aware of your own dalliance with the drug and how you overcame your addiction. Bravo, by the way. I'm a teetotaler myself."

"All the same, even though I'm no longer addicted, it can still affect me," Bugbear sighed.

"Exactly," the tall man said with a nod. "And considering that you've been talking up that little religion of yours wherever you go, we were quite aware of your rather remarkable abilities. Fortunately I had some of the serum with me when we found you."

Bugbear rolled his eyes and snarled. "Yes, how fortunate. Fortunate also that you were able to find two sticks to rub together so you could burn perhaps the most valuable and extensive collection of ancient manuscripts in existence!"

The tall man glanced over his shoulder to look at the bonfire. "Are you upset?" he said with an arched brow.

"Yes!" Bugbear barked. "There are records in that library that might provide clues to the identity of an ancient enemy recently resurrected!"

"An enemy? Of your kind? Or humankind?"

"Of all kind!" Bugbear said. "Please! For the love of sanity, stop them!"

The tall man regarded Bugbear for a moment, then looked to the men piling parchments and books onto the fire. "The burning of words does seem backwards, doesn't it?" He stepped towards the men and waved them off. "That's enough of that! Leave the rest for intelligence officers to review!"

One of the soldiers saluted the tall man. "But, Sir, Colonel Rutledge's orders were…"

"Colonel Rutledge is in charge of the military aspects of this operation," the tall man broke in. "I manage the operation itself, as ordered by the Vice President. Are you questioning Theodore Roosevelt, soldier?"

"No, Sir!" the soldier said with a sudden snap to extra-alertness. He then turned to bark out the order to the other soldiers, who quickly abandoned their sacrilege.

Bugbear plopped his rear onto a nearby stump and let out a grateful sigh. "I only hope we aren't too late. If the Coranieid records were already destroyed, I may never uncover the true nature of the enemy… until it's too late."

The tall man smiled to Bugbear, his teeth perfect and straight, but stained by a long romance with coffee. "My apologies. As I said, our understanding of the fey races is limited, and some of my colleagues are a bit uneasy when it comes to different cultures… Especially after Brenen's attack on one of our garrisons outside of Toledo."

"Brenen attacked you first?" Bugbear said with a frown.

"Indeed," the tall man replied. "A small raiding party. Killed a good two dozen of our men, shooting them with arrows from the brush. We caught a few of them, found out where they came from... although all denied having attacked us. Hard denying the Áes dána arrows sticking out of our men's backs though."

Bugbear eyed the tall man suspiciously. "You seem rather generous with your information, good sir."

"Because I'm expecting the same from you, Mister Bugbear," the tall man answered with a nod. "You're used to collaborating with humans after all, aren't you?"

"Those I know and trust," Bugbear said with a sour smirk.

"Then know that my name is Howard Asherby, Special Agent in the United States Secret Service," the tall man said. "The trust shall have to come with time, I suppose."

"If the trust ever comes at all, Mister Asherby," Bugbear said, offering his hand as the shackles fell away.

Asherby regarded Bugbear with subtle alarm. "Your chains? How did you...?"

"You have temporarily stripped me of my ability to use Non-Logic," Bugbear answered as he held up a small sliver of metal, "not my ability to use lock picks."

Asherby smiled, clearly admiring his opponent's resourcefulness. "I am glad our paths have crossed, Mister Bugbear. I am more than happy to allow you to pick through the remains of Brenen's library, if you will but answer a few questions."

Bugbear looked from Asherby to the pile of books and back to Asherby. "A fair trade," Bugbear shrugged. "Until I find a way to escape your clutches all together."

Asherby's smile widened. "I like you, sir. If you ever get tired of serving King Martin," he said, "there's always a position for you in the United States Intelligence Services."

"You seem to think that serving one precludes serving the other," Bugbear grunted. "You may well find that there is more honor and glory in serving everyone and everything, than in limiting yourself to but one master."

Asherby scowled and huffed, shifting weight from one foot to the other in some strange dance of indecision. "About those questions," he finally stammered. Asherby motioned to one of his lieutenants who produced a parchment and pen for the taking of notes. "Your King Martin is quite ambitious," Asherby started. "Building railroads and making alliances... without the permission of the United States government. What are his goals for this so-called Kingdom of Willow Prairie?"

Bugbear cocked his head. "To tell you the truth, I don't rightly know. Preservation mostly, I suppose."

"Preservation of what?" Asherby asked.

The goblin frowned, searching his scattered brain for some stray bits of inspiration he might cobble together into a suitable answer. "The purple banners of ageless, imagined empires!" he finally blurted, his tongue suddenly seized with inspiration. "The tantalizing treasures of childhood make-believe! The shimmering illusions of what might be!"

Asherby regarded the wild-eyed little man with distrust. "What do you mean by that?"

"Dreams, Mister Asherby!" Bugbear laughed. "Dreams! That is what King Martin wishes to preserve!"

Asherby tugged at his gun belt as he swayed with agitation. "Dreams can turn into nightmares awful quick, Mister Bugbear."

Nightmares. The word drove a spike into Bugbear's mind, causing him to recall the visions that had once guided and haunted him.

They had shown him the rise of the Shadow Smith, as well as his own fall into addiction and delirium. But both the Smith and the addiction had been defeated. Still the visions had not returned since. Perhaps Bugbear had outgrown them. Or perhaps the ancient enemy had already acted against him, casting some sinister spell that dulled his abilities to perceive the future.

Bugbear shook the worries from his head, before clearing his voice. *"The Sandman sleeps, whilst the dreamer weeps,"* he intoned in a most official way.

"What's that supposed to mean?" Asherby said, his face washed in confusion.

"A line from an old goblin playwright named Twistroot," Bugbear explained. "I have no idea what it means. But perhaps it would make us both the wiser to ponder it."

Asherby's face was ambushed by a sudden grin. "I've been making a habit of smiling since meeting you, Mister Bugbear," he chuckled. "I've got to admit, it's not something I enjoy. If you could limit your answers to matters at hand..."

"Limit," Bugbear snorted. "What a depressing little word." Bugbear sighed, his head wobbling upon his neck like a melon balanced upon a feather. "Very well. I shall avoid any answers that might cause your face to grin-split."

"You mentioned some ancient enemy," Asherby said. "How did you hear of it? What do you know so far?"

"Last year," Bugbear said as he commenced pacing in the way that storytellers are apt, "shortly after the two worlds were reunited, King Martin, his queen, my cousin, a young human-animal patchwork named Riley, and I confronted a creature. This creature, known as the Shadow Smith, was actually but a shadow of a greater threat. He was their herald, if you will. The one who would prepare the world for their coming. All I know of the Shadow Smith's masters is what I have learned from the dragon brides and from a lone survivor of the Coranieid Empire. The enemy we face is a terrible and powerful evil. Once they opposed the dragons themselves. In fact, the dragons had to sacrifice their own existence on this plane to eliminate them." Bugbear ceased his pacing and looked up to Asherby, his leathery face drawn tight with concern. "What these beings are called, where they hail from, or how they have returned, I do not know. But the Coranieid race once served them. That is why I'm hoping their records might hold some clues."

"Congratulations," Asherby grumbled. "You've stopped making me smile."

"You'll allow me to go on my way then?"

"Not yet," the tall man said with a shake of his head. "You can study the records in our camp just as easily as you can back in Willow Prairie. In fact, I reckon you'll be safer here."

"As your prisoner," Bugbear grunted.

"I told you before, Mister Bugbear, I like you. I don't hold people I like prisoner. I do, however, keep them close at hand if I feel they're in danger."

"Had you not injected me with that cursed concoction, I wouldn't be in danger," Bugbear protested.

"True enough," Asherby said with a bow. "And seeing as how I am responsible for your current situation, I insist you remain under my protection until the banderberry root has worn off. Fair enough?"

Bugbear let out a cool, bitter breath as he glared at Asherby through half-closed eyes. In many ways, the tall man reminded Bugbear of Brenen... at once accommodating and confrontational. But there was also the stink of sincerity about Asherby, something the Áes dána king lacked. The goblin wanted to like him... to trust him. But it was a difficult chore. His mind swam with suspicions and danced with doubts. Even if Asherby was sincere, was there any guarantee his comrades would follow the same creed? Could they not have their own agenda? Their own politics? And yet, at this point, his tie to Non-Logic severed, Bugbear had little choice but to trust the tall man in the black suit.

"No. Not fair at all," Bugbear finally grunted. "But reasonable given the circumstances."

Asherby nodded. "I'll have the books taken to your tent."

Bugbear arched a brow. "Accommodations are to be provided then?"

"Yes," Asherby said with a sardonic grin. "Although I'm afraid you might find quarters a bit cramped."

"How so?" Bugbear asked.

A shrill voice shattered the conversation, pulling all attention to a small army tent pitched a few yards from where Asherby and Bugbear stood. "What have you done to my face?"

"Oh," Bugbear said with closed eyes and a satisfied smile. "I smell irony in the air."

Asherby looked to Bugbear with a perplexed scowl before rushing off towards the tent. Bugbear danced behind the tall man, his laughter almost a song as it trilled from his smiling lips.

Asherby pulled the tent flap aside and entered, Bugbear ducking under the tall man's arm and scampering inside. Several army medics held Brenen down on a cot as he squirmed and writhed like a worm on a hook. The left side of his face was bandaged, and the rest of his face was washed in wide brushstrokes of terror. Bugbear's eyes immediately lit with a mix of surprise and amusement.

"You are responsible for this!" Brenen cursed as his eyes fell upon Bugbear. "You led these savages to my kingdom! Because of you I'm unseelie!"

"I would love nothing more than to take responsibility for your current state," Bugbear replied as he approached the bedside and casually browsed through Brenen's medical charts. "But I'm afraid this is a severe case of 'karmic comeuppance'." Bugbear paused a moment as he absorbed the words on the chart. He smiled knowingly as he placed the chart back on the bedside. "As I recall your cousin, Queen Rígan, was also tragically disfigured some years ago. Poor girl ended losing an arm after her horse threw her. They never did find out how that metal shard got under her saddle."

Brenen strained against the soldiers. "What are you implying?"

"Nothing. I'm merely glad that you were there to assume the throne when she was declared 'unseelie' and banished." Bugbear paused and patted Brenen's hand with condescending concern. "Too bad you weren't able to maintain order when the Áes dána empire fractured soon after. Perhaps your replacement will be able to repair the damage."

With a wild roar Brenen broke free from the soldiers, grasping Bugbear by the collar and hoisting him in the air. "I'll kill you!"

"Corporal!" Asherby barked. "Restrain that man!"

The soldiers rushed forward, but before they could seize Brenen, Bugbear snapped his foot up into Brenen's face, the heel striking the Áes dána king quite sharply on the chin. Brenen collapsed, and Bugbear dropped to the ground unharmed save for a wrinkled shirt.

The soldiers regarded Bugbear with caution as they moved to recover the unconscious Brenen. Asherby approached the goblin, his brow furrowed as he watched the men place Brenen back in his cot.

"Non-Logical Thought?" Asherby asked as he placed a hand on Brenen's forehead.

"No," Bugbear said. The goblin took up Brenen's chart, placing it discretely in his coat-of-many-pockets. "*Big Practical Feet*. You see, we goblins tend to travel quite a bit, giving us perhaps the sturdiest feet of any race. So, lifting me up to his level, was a grave mistake for good King Brenen. Like the old goblin saying goes: *It's a fool who puts his fate in a goblin's feet.*"

Asherby smirked as he turned towards Bugbear. "So, what is this 'unseemly' nonsense?"

"The word is 'unseelie'." Bugbear walked to the tent flap and motioned Asherby through. "The Áes dána are a very proud and vain race." Bugbear followed Asherby outside as they surveyed the camp. "Even the slightest imperfection results in banishment to what is known as *the unseelie court*. To be unseelie is a shame so great that these outcasts have hidden themselves away from any and all eyes. Only another Áes dána would know how to find the court."

"Seems rather harsh," Asherby said.

"All cultures have their unsavory traditions," Bugbear replied. "That charm you wear about your neck, for example. A knight slaying a dragon? That would be considered a very tasteless image among my kind."

Asherby held up the small medal he wore about his neck and examined it. "It's Saint George, the patron saint of soldiers. The dragon he slew was an evil, plague-bearing serpent."

"Not likely," Bugbear scoffed as he stopped near the pile of books, absently picking one bound in red leather. "Dragons were teachers and protectors. They're about as likely to spread plague as humans are peace."

Asherby chuckled slightly. "Let's be fair. Maybe there were some good dragons on your world, but that doesn't mean a few bad ones couldn't have gotten onto mine."

"The dragons in your folklore and legends are simply corrupted memories of the time before the Great Sundering. True dragons were part of Annwfn, and they vanished long, long ago."

"Well," Asherby smirked, "most of the dragons we have around here these days sit on Congressional committees."

Bugbear paid little heed to Asherby's words. He flipped through the book, his eyes darting here and there, absorbing random words and sentences. "Yes," he said with a sudden outburst of discovery. "This is the book."

"What book?" Asherby said, his face fogged with confusion.

"The book with answers," Bugbear answered.

"That's it? You simply pick up a book, flip through it, and you know it's the one you need?"

Bugbear handed the book to Asherby. "Read the inscription on the inside cover."

Asherby opened the book and read the inscription: *"Dear Bugbear, this is the book with the answers. Do take care of it. And tell Asherby to mind the arrow."* Asherby looked up from the book, his brow crooked with confusion. "Arrow?"

Like an airborne viper, a rune-tattooed arrow buried into Asherby's calf, sending him down to one knee. "Sonuva...!" the tall man exclaimed as Bugbear rushed to his side. "Ambush!" he yelled to his men. "Open fire!"

Soon the camp erupted in arrows, gunfire, and rage. Áes dána warriors charged into the clearing, swords drawn and war cries unleashed. The soldiers fired their rifles and pistols, the smell of burnt powder clouding eyes and stinging nostrils. Bugbear urged the limping Asherby out of the clearing and into the forest. Asherby struggled, tugging his way back towards his men. But Bugbear was insistent, pulling the tall man forward with a strength that belied his stunted body.

"I can't leave my men!" Asherby protested.

"You are wounded," Bugbear argued as he continued dragging the stubborn soldier into the brush. "At least let me remove that arrow before you limp into martyrdom!"

"No," Asherby blurted. "I..."

With a scream wrought from nightmares, and a bright light born of revelation, something strange and alien hit the center of the encampment, scattering the human soldiers with a bright and unfettered explosion of energy.

"Banshee ball!" Bugbear exclaimed. "They have alchemists with them, Asherby! We must leave now!"

Blinded, crippled, and confused, Asherby nodded and allowed Bugbear to pull him off into the brush. Behind them men screamed and strange magic devoured the landscape.

Bugbear grumbled as he glanced back through the haze of his retreat, "Can't I get through one bloody day without someone shooting at me?"

CHAPTER 4
TARGET PRACTICE

Manchester took a deep breath, exhaled, and squeezed the trigger. The hammer fell, the powder ignited, the bullet flew, and the empty can of beans fell off the log. The king spun the pistol in his hand and returned it to the holster.

"Your aim has improved," Maga said, as she came from behind him, her footfalls barely audible on the forest trail.

Manchester turned and smiled to her. He ran an uncertain hand into his tangle of black hair. "More the pistols than me, I imagine. Gift from Tudmire. Dwarf-forged custom 'twelve-shooters'. Never could have made a 100 yard shot like that with regular pistols. Well beyond what I was able to shoot as a boy in my parents' backyard."

"Well, you've grown up to be well beyond a mere boy, haven't you?" Maga said, coming up behind him and placing her head on his shoulder in a wistful, pensive manner.

Manchester turned about and placed his hands upon Maga's shoulders. "You seem sad, Maga. I realize we have a lot to deal with lately with Pawe and the Áes dána, but..."

Maga broke away. She shook her head and sighed. "I've felt a heaviness in my heart that I can't explain. Something about the world seems different lately. As if every moment is leading into another greater, more critical moment, building and growing into an event more monumental than the birth of the universe."

"Your aim has improved."

Manchester smiled and suppressed a small laugh. "You sound like Bugbear."

Maga frowned. "No I don't. You wouldn't laugh at Bugbear." And with a dismissive wave of her hand she stormed down the trail.

"Maga," Manchester called after her. "I didn't mean...." As the dragon bride disappeared into the brush, Manchester stopped, grunted and turned about to trudge down the trail toward the fallen bean can.

There was a time when he would have been certain he was at fault. When they first met his tongue was thick with blunders, and every inch of him seemed saturated with inelegance. But Maga had always been forgiving of and enchanted by his missteps and mistakes. Manchester was certainly a different man now... more confident, less awkward. But recently Maga too had changed. Something dark and deep held hostage her bright spirit. Perhaps she fretted over the escape of the Barghest. Or she might have been concerned about Bugbear's disappearance. She could have even been worried about something more mundane, such as Riley's progress in school. Considering he was a patchwork of dog, cat, and boy, Riley acclimated quite well to the actual studies. But his social interactions were yet tainted by his animal nature. Just the other day Manchester and Maga had been called in by the teacher over an incident involving the release of a live rat in the schoolhouse. *"Everyone brings her apples,"* Riley explained. *"We were only trying to be original."* Yet Maga had laughed when she heard Riley's excuse, letting Manchester glimpse just a splinter of her old self.

Since then, though, she seemed steeped in worry and anguish. It was as if in being a part of her life, Manchester had chained her to the ground.

As Manchester placed the can back on the log, behind him he heard the stamping of hooves on dirt. He spun about, drawing both his custom pistols.

"Easy, Mister," the mounted cavalry officer said with upraised hand. Behind him rode a dozen more armed men, many wounded and all rather unkempt. "We intend no harm."

Manchester lowered his pistols, but kept them free of the holsters. "Then what do you intend?"

The officer swayed in his saddle a moment, as if debating whether to part with the truth, or spin a lie. "Two days ago my men and I were separated from our company during a battle. Since then we've engaged in a few skirmishes with hostile forces. You can probably tell by our current state that those skirmishes haven't gone well for us. We'd be mighty grateful if you'd allow us to tend to our wounded and rest a spell in your town."

Manchester looked to the officer with suspicion. "You know who I am?"

"Been briefed on you, sir," the officer nodded. "Royalty doesn't pop up in the middle of Indiana without being noticed."

Manchester snorted and gave a crooked grin. "I suppose not." Manchester looked over the soldiers, his gaze traveling from one dirty face to the next. Boys mostly. Frightened, wounded boys. Manchester looked to the officer. He could tell by the uniform his rank was Lieutenant. And he could tell by the demeanor his experience was little. "Very well, you and your men can stay as long as you need. But I'll have to ask you to turn in your weapons until you're ready to leave."

The Lieutenant balked. "I can't agree to that, Sir. We're soldiers. We need...."

"You need to rest. You don't need guns for that."

"Unacceptable," the Lieutenant insisted. "A United States Army officer cannot allow his men to surrender their firearms."

Manchester grinned. He glanced back into the thick woods behind them. "Loomis!"

Trees groaned and shook. The ground rumbled. Three large shadows devoured the forest. And at the birth of those shadows stood three purple-hued brutes, at least twelve feet tall and half as wide.

"Gentlemen," Manchester said as he motioned to the giants, "my bodyguards."

"Ogres!" the Lieutenant blurted. His men fumbled in their saddles and holsters for rifles and pistols.

"Easy, son," Manchester laughed. "Loomis and his brothers won't hurt you. And even so, from what I hear nothing short of a buffalo rifle can stop an ogre. Near as I can tell, only one of your men is in possession of such a weapon. And I suspect I can get off a shot on him before he can even free it from the scabbard."

"You're a traitor to your country, sir," the Lieutenant said with a scowl.

Manchester's face froze into a stone glare. "I love my country, Lieutenant. Which is why I enjoy educating my fellow Americans on the virtues of prudence every chance I get." Manchester holstered his pistols and walked up to the officer, patting the muzzle of his horse as he fed it a piece of hard candy. "You have three choices, son. You can ride out of here with your weapons, and hope you get to Brockville before gangrene sets in. You can try fighting your way into Willow Prairie, which I guarantee will result in losing your weapons permanently, a much longer hospital stay, and your horses being eaten by my bodyguards."

The Lieutenant and his men warily glanced to Loomis and his brothers, wincing as they saw the drool dripping from their grinning maws.

"Or you can turn in your weapons and enjoy some good ol' fashioned Hoosier hospitality." Manchester smiled, hoping to take some of the sting out of the dishonor.

The Lieutenant let out an exasperated huff of air. Then he looked to Manchester, his face drawn into a knot of conflict. "You'll return them when we're ready to leave?"

"I'll even supply you with fresh ammunition." Manchester removed a bullet from his gun belt and handed it to the Lieutenant. The Lieutenant received it with trepidation and suspicion. "Dwarf-forged bullets," Manchester said as the officer examined the bullet. "Almost five times the velocity of your ammunition, ten times as strong, and will improve your accuracy nearly seventy percent. What with the trade agreements between Willow Prairie and the Winestain Mountains, I can have five crates here before you and your men get fresh bandages."

The Lieutenant weighed the bullet in his hand. Then with a smirk and a nod, he tossed it back to Manchester. "I apologize for questioning your patriotism, King Martin," the Lieutenant said as he removed his rifle from its scabbard and handed it off to one of the ogres. His men did likewise with their pistols, rifles, swords, and knives, some grumbling more than others. The Lieutenant urged his mount forward, regarding Manchester as he passed. "By the way, name's Arthur Pope."

"Lieutenant Pope," Manchester said with a casual salute, "welcome to Willow Prairie."

Nigel and Dubbin walked beside the men as they rode down the trail towards town. Manchester waved for Loomis to stay behind. The big ogre knelt down on one knee lending his ear to the king.

"Whats wordings you has, boss?"

"Bring them around to the east side of town, by Doc Glenn's. He can tend to their wounds, and they can set up their tents in the empty lot next door." Manchester pulled the ogre closer. "Whatever you do, do not let them near Mother Twitchett's. If they get wind of our Áes dána guests...."

"Smasherings aplenty," Loomis said with an understanding nod. "Me brothers and me be learnering many a usefulness thingy of diplomatics on recently visitations with Great Ogre Father. We be very cleverful and guiling with these army folk."

Manchester patted Loomis on the shoulder. "As solid as the rock you resemble, old friend," he laughed.

"Always inner your services, him Majestic." Loomis rose, but wagged a finger as he looked down to Manchester with sudden irritation. "But please not to be spreadering falsitudes of ogre horsey eatsings. Be badly for genteel image Ogre Father wishering to be reflectsing on ogre-kin."

Manchester nodded. "Understood." The king fell in beside Loomis as they walked the trail into town.

Tudmire threw the sauce pan against the wall, nearly splattering the king with fish sauce as he entered the kitchen. Manchester sidestepped the mess and dodged the various cooks, waiters, waitresses, maids, and other servants as they darted about the kitchen in a hectic cyclone of culinary chaos.

"Blast those finicky Áes dána palates!" Tudmire cursed as he slammed another pan onto the stovetop. He began dumping ingredients into the pan, his eyes almost as red and angry as the flames that shot up around the grill.

"Our guests proving difficult?" Manchester asked, coming up behind his seneschal with an exasperated sigh.

"Difficult?" Tudmire snorted as he turned about waving a wooden spoon before the king. "They've sent back every dish I've set before them! Outlandish!" Tudmire turned back to the pan, stirring the contents with the kind of anger fanatics reserve for the torment of heathens. "Do you know how many culinary competitions I've won?" Tudmire asked, turning about to once again wave the wooden spoon at Manchester.

"Lots?" Manchester wagered as he evaded the splatters of sauce.

"None!" Tudmire barked as he turned back to the pan. "My creations were considered so phenomenal, so unearthly, so divine, that the Caer Coblyn Culinary Commission banned me from entering any competitions out of fairness to less accomplished chefs!" Tudmire spun about, waving the wooden spoon like a saber, scattering sauce everywhere. "But these self-important puff-n-preens think they're better than the finest fare to ever touch his Majesty's royal china!"

Manchester licked a splatter of sauce from his mustache and smacked his lips. "Clearly, their tongues are blind." Manchester gently guided Tudmire away from the stove, steering him towards the icebox. "So why waste your valuable time and skills, when you can simply serve them last night's beef stew?"

Tudmire's face balled up in wrinkled confusion. "Leftovers? You expect me to serve them leftovers?" The goblin's fat face loosened into a wild laugh. "Ha! Excellent! I'll even have it served to them cold!" Tudmire tapped a waitress and motioned her to the big pot of stew in the icebox. "Please serve our esteemed Áes dána visitors this fine *Norwegian Walrus Potage!*"

The waitress gave Tudmire a quizzical look, but then shrugged and hefted the pot out of the icebox.

"If they try to return it, dump it on their heads!" Tudmire called after her.

Manchester placed a hand on Tudmire's shoulder as he bent down to speak secretly. "I need you to get in touch with your dwarf friends in the Winestain Mountains. We'll need about five more crates of their new ammunition."

Tudmire shrugged. "I can have a messenger out today. Should have them on the next train around two days from now. Unless our eastbound deliveries are having as much difficulty as our westbound arrivals. The 3:10 from Toledo is three days late." Tudmire wiped his hands on his apron and slid closer to Manchester. "May I ask why you're in need of so much ammunition?" he whispered.

Manchester pulled Tudmire closer. "I'm allowing some U.S.

soldiers to recover in Willow Prairie for a while. I offered them the ammunition in exchange for turning in their guns during their stay."

Tudmire shook his head. "Dangerous, your majesty. If the Áes dána find out you're harboring American soldiers...."

"Not to worry. Loomis and his brothers have escorted them to Doc Glenn's on the other side of town."

Tudmire winced and gulped.

"What's wrong?" Manchester asked, panic edging his voice.

"One of the Áes dána complained of stomach cramps after tasting my buttered sleels, so I..."

"You didn't...."

"... sent him over to Doc Glenn's...."

"Tudmire, you're fired!" Manchester blurted as he darted out the door and into the street.

The kitchen staff stopped their labors and looked to Tudmire. The goblin scowled and violently waved his hands at them. "He was joking! Back to work!"

CHAPTER 5
ON THE MOVE

Maga found the bureaucracy the most mind-numbing part of being queen. Several months ago she and Martin had set aside a small portion of Willow Prairie's recent windfall to rebuild the town library. It seemed a simple enough affair at the time... just reconstruct a building to hold books on shelves. But with affluence came foolishness. Every somebody, nobody, and busybody in town wanted to put his or her stamp on this new project. As Maga went over the plans with the foreman, she became aware of just what a complicated and frustrating stamp collection she had on her hands.

"So, we figure the statue of Bugbear can go on the lawn right in front of the steps," the foreman said as he pointed to the empty lot where the once-and-future library had and would be.

"There will be no statue of Bugbear," Maga said between gritted teeth.

"I s'pose that will leave more room for the carousel," the foreman said, nodding to his men, who nodded in agreement as they ate their sandwiches and drank their coffee.

"No carousel," Maga said, her voice a low growl.

The foreman shrugged and sifted through the pages of plans. "Indoor pool?"

"No."

"Betting parlor?"

"No."

"Secret network of underground tunnels?"

Maga grabbed the plans from the foreman and threw them on the ground. "Listen," she hissed. "For the next few days, the king and I are going to be in the forest outside of town hunting the Barghest. While we are gone, you shall build a library. A simple library, with shelves, and desks, and chairs. And books. Lots and lots of books."

The foreman nodded his head and looked to Maga with an agreeable grin. "Understood. But do you want the billiards hall on the first or second floor?"

Maga placed her hand on the hilt of her sword, and was preparing a stream of such devastating threats that they would have sent an ogre to the washtub with a pair of soiled trousers. But the foreman was spared such indignity, for just as Maga parted her lips to unleash her venom, Manchester bolted past.

"Excuse me," Maga said, her anger replaced with curiosity as she fell in behind her frantic husband.

Manchester had never been a good runner. He had told Maga how illness had bound him to bed for much of his childhood, robbing him of recess races and games of tag. But now, as he ran through the streets of Willow Prairie, dodging horses, carriages, and dwarven automobiles, Maga had no doubt he was making up for every inch he had missed all those years past. Even with the advantages of her dragon bride heritage, she was barely a match for his panic-fueled pace.

"Where are you off to in such a hurry?" she asked, finally catching up to him.

"Áes dána," Manchester huffed. "Food poisoning," he puffed. "Soldiers," he gasped. "Diplomatic nightmare," he sputtered.

Maga sighed and put out a hand to slow the king to a trot. "What are you on about?"

Manchester stopped, placing his hands on his knees as he struggled to regain his breath. "For God's sake," he wheezed, "why did you let me get in such bad shape?"

Maga laughed. She looked into her exhausted husband's eyes and saw a sudden relief melt his anxiety. Something turned in her stomach, reminding her just how harsh she had been to him of late. She blamed most of her ill mood on the dull and dreary duties that weighed on her. But she now realized the same duties weighed on him as well. Together they needed to smile more.

"What's wrong?" Maga asked, helping Manchester stand.

"An Áes dána is going to Doc Glenn's," he said, as his breath returned.

"And you're trying to beat him there before he takes all the lollypops?"

"No. I'm trying to get there before he gets beaten by the American soldiers I let into town."

"You let soldiers into town?" Maga gasped. "Are you insane?"

"They were wounded," Manchester said, rubbing his forehead with frustration. "They're my people, Maga. Wouldn't you do the same for your sisters?"

"Maybe so," Maga said, placing a hand along Manchester's cheek. "But my sisters aren't on the verge of war with the Áes dána empire." She shook her head and sighed as she playfully slapped him. "Come on."

Maga darted forward like a doe, and Manchester tumbled after her like a dolt. Before they could make too much progress, however, they were met with a hail of howls, shouts, and jeers. As they rounded the corner to Doc Glenn's house, Maga watched with wide disbelieving eyes as Loomis and his brothers held six of the soldiers up by the scruffs of their necks. An officer had evaded the ogres' grasps and was in the midst of hogtying a rather agitated Áes dána nobleman with a length of twine. The officer nodded to Manchester and Maga as they approached.

"Caught a spy for you, sir," he said to Manchester with a crooked grin.

"I am not a spy!" the nobleman protested. "Tell this barbarian to untie me, King Martin! Or do you intend to rescind your offer of asylum?"

Manchester sighed, took up Maga's hand, and used it to slap himself.

"Asylum?" the soldier said as he stood and looked to Manchester with outrage. "You're harboring this scum?"

"And twenty of my brothers," the Áes dána laughed.

"That's why you wanted us to turn in our weapons," the soldier scowled. "You are a traitor! You set a trap for us!"

"I did no such thing, Pope" Manchester growled. "I have no idea what exactly is going on between the U.S. Army and the Áes dána empire, but I have a town to protect. There was no way I was going to allow armed men into town knowing the animosity brought about by recent events."

"Use all the pretty words you want to explain your treason, 'King Martin'," Pope spat, "but history loathes liars."

Manchester fumed. Maga placed a hand on his shoulder, but she could tell he was beyond appeasement.

The king unbuckled his gun belt and let it drop to the dusty street. Shaking off Maga's hand, he lumbered over to Pope, his eyes slits of smoldering anger. "Now I'm unarmed too, boy," Manchester sneered. "You suppose you can subdue me as easily as you did that fop there?"

"I did put up a bit of a fight," the Áes dána muttered as he strained at the twine.

"I ain't going to fight you, sir," Pope grumbled. "I'm a trained soldier. Wouldn't be fair."

"That your excuse?" Manchester laughed. He turned about to address the gathering crowd. "Well, you know, history loathes a coward as much as a liar!"

As Manchester turned back around to Pope, the enraged Lieutenant let loose a lightning bolt with a fist at the end. The crowd gasped as Manchester flew back some three feet, falling onto his rear in the dust. Manchester held back Maga as she moved forward, hand on her sword hilt. He smiled and wiped the specks of blood from his mouth as he got to his feet. Maga looked to him with disapproval.

"The king should not engage in combat like this," she said.

"Then I'll abdicate till I'm done taking this boy to school."

Manchester danced and weaved his way back to Pope, his hands up in boxing position. Maga stood back, shaking her head and sighing. Manchester could be a capable combatant under the right circumstances. In the past he had successfully engaged and defeated bullies, patchworks, and even ogres. But in their occasional sparing sessions, Maga had noticed a recklessness and sloppiness a more cautious fighter like Pope could easily exploit. She did not fear for Manchester's safety as much as his ego and reputation... a reputation that became increasingly endangered as more and more people gathered about to watch the unfolding battle.

Pope unleashed another punch, which Manchester blocked. The king countered with a quick jab to the gut, sending Pope doubling over. Manchester used the momentum to pull Pope's face down into his upraised knee. The Lieutenant fell back, staggering as blood spurted from his nose. Manchester lunged forward, lifting the still stunned Pope off the ground. The king rolled over, flying into the air with Pope held in a bear hug. They both fell to the ground, Pope taking the brunt of the impact.

Maga watched with wonder as her husband knelt over Pope, pummeling him with a hailstorm of fists. Her mouth fell open, partly in awe of the pure, brutal beauty, and partly in guilt for her lack of faith. The crowd hummed around her, ever growing. The other Áes dána dignitaries had arrived, dripping with cold beef stew, for some unknown reason. Tudmire wormed his way into the throng as well, mesmerized like everyone else as their king unleashed a kind of punishment seldom seen outside the arenas of ancient Rome.

With a victorious groan, Manchester stood, Pope rolling in the dirt beneath him, bloodied and barely conscious. He waved to the ogres.

"Release the soldiers," he grunted. "Let them tend to their Lieutenant."

Loomis and his brothers nodded, dropping their captives to the ground. The soldiers found their legs and quickly scampered away from the ogres, towards their fallen comrade.

Manchester staggered to the water pump in front of Doc Glenn's house. Maga hurried over to him, swelling with pride and relief.

"Martin," she said as the king splashed the cool water into his face, "that was...."

"That was stupid," Manchester snorted with a crooked smile. He turned to Maga and fell into her with a hard, deep hug. "Sorry if I get you wet."

Maga laughed as the water from his beard trickled down her neck. She kissed him softly on the cheek, and nibbled lightly on his earlobe. "You are a devious and cunning magician," she whispered.

Manchester released her from the hug, his face melting into a frown as the water dripped off his chin. "We need to end this."

Maga looked to him with uncertainty. "End what?"

"Whatever it is that's stirred up the Army and the Áes dána. We need to get to the bottom of this." Manchester took Maga's face in his hands and kissed her forehead. "I'm sorry I laughed at you earlier. You were right. Monumental events are being moved against us. It's time to rise up and meet these events before they overwhelm us."

"Where do we start?" Maga asked, looking into his eyes.

"Follow me." Manchester took her hand and walked over to his discarded gun belt. He picked it up, placed it back on his waist, and buckled it as he walked over to Pope and the other soldiers. The soldiers frowned and stood to the side, letting their wounded commander stand to face the king. Maga watched cautiously as she bent down to cut the twine holding the Áes dána diplomat.

"You can have your weapons back," Manchester said to Pope. "But I'm going to ask a favor of you."

"What might that be?" Pope snorted.

"I want you and any men you can spare to accompany us to Washington."

The Lieutenant smirked. "Why would you want to go to Washington?"

Manchester stroked his still damp beard. "I plan to seek an audience with the President of the United States."

CHAPTER 6
REFUGEES

Asherby winced as he tried to find a comfortable way to prop his wounded leg on the rock. Bugbear smirked as he cleaned his hands and several small instruments and tools in the nearby stream.

"Would have been a much cleaner and less painful operation if only..."

"If only I hadn't robbed you of your connection to Non-Logical Thought," Asherby interrupted with a grunt and a sigh.

"Ah," Bugbear said, drying his hands on his britches and placing the instruments back into his coat-of-many-pockets, "we've developed a rapport. Excellent. Should make traveling together much more bearable."

The goblin waddled over to sit on a rock next to Asherby. He removed a satchel containing a small loaf of bread and a wedge of cheese. He cut off a portion of the bread and a slice of the cheese and offered them to Asherby.

"Hungry?"

Asherby accepted the offer, shaking his head with disbelief. "How much does that coat of yours carry, anyway?"

"Everything I need, and nothing less," Bugbear shrugged as if the answer was obvious.

Asherby chuckled between mouthfuls of bread and cheese. He looked to the sun as it waned in the west, staining the sky purple and yellow. "Night soon," he grunted. "Got any blankets in that coat of yours?"

"No," Bugbear said as he packed the rest of the food away. "We should keep moving anyway."

"At night? With my wound?"

"Well," Bugbear said, standing up and walking over to the brush,

"I'd suggest leaving the wound behind." The goblin sorted through various twigs and branches until coming across one that seemed to meet his criteria. "But it seems to have grown quite fond of your leg." He threw the stick to Asherby.

Asherby caught the stick and looked to it with uncertainty. "I don't think this will hold my weight."

"Don't you recognize it?" Bugbear laughed. "Comes from the humble banderberry tree. The roots may be treacherous, but I've yet to find a sturdier wood."

Asherby stood, cautiously testing his weight on the new cane. "Seems sturdy enough," he observed as he hobbled around the small clearing.

Bugbear watched Asherby with a crooked grin. "Yes," he said "You can see now how banderberry can be used for more than just cruelly robbing one of his..."

"Connection to Non-Logical Thought," Asherby sighed. "Okay. It was a stale tune the first time I heard it, and it's not getting any fresher." The tall man hobbled over to Bugbear, who stood with arms crossed at the trail. "I apologize from the bottom of my bureaucratic heart. Can we drop it now?"

"Yes," Bugbear nodded. "Once I find a new tune. Which would be much easier if someone hadn't robbed me of my connection to Non-Logical Thought."

Bugbear offered a sarcastic smile as he skipped down the trail ahead of Asherby. Asherby fell in behind with a grumble and stumble. "Going to be a long night."

As the purple and yellow sky dimmed to navy and gray, the forest grew thick with nocturnal sounds... crickets, frogs, and other less familiar things. Asherby's nerves did a savage dance along the back of his neck. Instinctively he reached for the handle of his pistol, only to find an empty holster. He closed his eyes and winced as he remembered having one of the privates clean it for him back at camp. Fortunately, he still carried the one-shot derringer in his vest pocket, and the Bowie knife in his boot.

"Where are you leading us?" he asked Bugbear as the goblin peered about the forest.

"Forward," the little man replied.

"Could you be a little more specific?"

"Yes. Yes. I believe I could," Bugbear replied as he suddenly removed the book from his coat and began reading.

Asherby groaned, the pain from his wound and the confusion from his companion hitting him with a double dose of misery. He had not been particularly comfortable with his assignment to investigate the *"Fey Situation"*, as the government had called it. But Vice President Roosevelt himself requested Asherby lead the expedition, so there was great political risk in turning down the command. Still, hobbling through the twilight forest with a demented goblin as his guide, Asherby was quite certain banishment from the Washington power circles would have been a much safer and more comfortable fate.

A snapping twig set his soldiers instincts on edge. Asherby tugged the oblivious Bugbear to a halt as he removed his derringer and peered into the brush ahead. He motioned for Bugbear to stay put as he hobbled forward, maintaining an awkward balance of weapon, wound, and banderberry cane.

With a huff like a dying steam engine, and just as much courtly grace, Brenen broke through onto the trail. He gasped, sputtered, and collapsed before Asherby. Asherby shook his head as he looked down at the disgraced Áes dána king.

"I assumed your subjects would have liberated you," Asherby

drawled as he placed his derringer back in his vest.

Brenen wheezed and whined as he dragged himself to his feet. "Those were not my subjects," he hissed. "They wore my colors and bore my banner, but they were not of my clan."

"Really?" Asherby turned to Bugbear who yet buried his nose in the mysterious tome. "What do you make of that?"

"Hmmmm? Yes. Fascinating." The goblin drifted further into his reading, dismissing Asherby all together with a long and disinterested hum.

Brenen snorted to Asherby. "I see you are wounded as well. Now you know what it is like to be unseelie."

"Hardly," Asherby said with a cutting smile. "My people will give me a medal for getting wounded in the line of duty."

Brenen frowned. "Your people have no concept of perfection and beauty."

Asherby scowled and turned away from the fallen king. He hobbled over to Bugbear, trying to nudge him out of his scholarly stupor. "Let's head out before we pick up any more stray idiots."

"I wrote this," Bugbear suddenly blurted as he lowered the book and looked to Asherby with wide, demented eyes.

"You wrote the book?"

"No!" Bugbear snarled. "The inscription in the front! I wrote it! It's my handwriting, no doubt about it."

"But how did you know I'd get hit with an arrow?"

"Because it had already happened," Bugbear said with an upraised finger.

"You know, you really need to learn to slow down when you're talking to me. I'm a smart man, but a sixth grade education only allows me to keep up with you for so long."

Bugbear smiled as he flipped through the book. He stopped as scribbles of red ink caught his eyes. "See here?" he said, pointing to the writing. "There are more notations! This one says *'What's next for you is past for me.'*"Bugbear slammed the book closed with a triumphant chuckle. "So you see, the only way I could have known that you were going to get hit by the arrow is if by the time I wrote this, it had already happened. Which means this book has somehow come to me by way of the future. Or perhaps I have come to the book by way of the past?"

Brenen broke between Bugbear and Asherby, his face a pasty mass of bitterness. "Are you two finished? Those Áes dána pretenders are still out there, you know."

As the Áes dána king droned on, Asherby noticed the last rays of the setting sun dancing on the edge of a blade in the brush behind Brenen. With a swift movement, Asherby removed his Bowie knife from the boot sheath and threw it into the bramble where it met some nearly invisible target. With a gurgle, rustle, and thud, the assassin fell out onto the trail.

With a gurgle, rustle, and thud, the assassin fell out onto the trail.

"Brenen has a point," Asherby said as he hobbled up to the corpse and removed his knife from the chest.

Bugbear scurried up to the dead body, his eyes scanning and examining it in the dull twilight. "Brenen, you said these weren't your men. How could you tell?"

Brenen wandered towards them, his shoulders rising in a lazy shrug. "They screamed, yelled, carried on like animals. My men are disciplined and civilized in battle. These maniacs were little better than humans."

Bugbear ran a twig along the edge of the dead warrior's blade.

"They turned on each other too," the goblin observed. "See how his blade is stained not only with red human blood, but blue Áes dána blood as well?"

"So? What does it all mean?" Asherby asked.

"It means we are quite fortunate that Brenen stumbled upon us," Bugbear said as he paged through the book.

"Why is that?" Brenen asked, his brow raised in suspicion.

Bugbear pointed to another handwritten notation in the book and read it aloud. *"Brenen shall lead you to the unseelie court, where answers shall be found."*

Brenen vigorously shook his head. "No! I shall not! I don't care how disfigured I may be. I won't join them!"

"Are you afraid of a reunion with some of your former rivals?" Bugbear asked with amusement in his voice. "I'm certain they would welcome you with open arms... and bared fangs."

Asherby coaxed Bugbear back as he moved towards Brenen with slightly more diplomatic intent. "You don't have to join them, Brenen. You just have to show us how to get there. While Bugbear rustles up whatever answers he thinks he'll find, you and I will stay well out of unseelie court's clutches."

"Oh, where's the fun in that?" Bugbear laughed.

"You aren't being very helpful here," Asherby spat.

Brenen lightly ran his fingertips along the bandages on his face. He closed his eyes and breathed in deeply. "I'll lead you half way and draw you a map to the rest."

"Fair enough," Asherby said with a sigh of relief. He turned to Bugbear with upraised eyebrows. "Fair enough?"

"Whatever gets us back on the trail again," Bugbear grumbled as he waved off Asherby and flipped through the book.

Asherby motioned Brenen to the trail. "Lead on."

Brenen stormed down the trail. Asherby followed... until he abruptly stumbled and fell on his face.

Bugbear turned the page. *"Tell Asherby to mind the groundhog hole,"* he read aloud.

Bugbear continued to study the book as Brenen led him and Asherby through the night-shrouded forest. Being a goblin, Bugbear's large eyes were quite efficient in making use of low light. He had little difficulty reading, even when the moonlight became veiled by drifting clouds. However, his large goblin ears could not help but hear the fumbling and stumbling Asherby, who seemed to have much more difficulty navigating at nighttime.

"Brenen,' Bugbear called ahead. "Perhaps we should stop for a bit of a rest? Our human companion seems ill-equipped for this hectic pace."

"I'll be fine," Asherby huffed. "I just need a torch or lantern so I can see where I'm limping."

"What a brilliant tactician you are," Brenen said sarcastically. *"Let's light a beacon so our enemies will be able to find us!"*

"Like your muttering about *indignities* and *conspiracies* hasn't been a dinner bell for every predator in the forest," Bugbear spat.

"You know," Asherby groaned, "this wounded leg is turning out to be a more agreeable traveling companion than either one of you."

"Fine!" Brenen exclaimed. "I'm done with both of you! I'll take my chances in...."

Something moaned behind them. An eerie, deep, bone-rattling moan... like a nightmare escaping a madman's mind.

"What was that?" Asherby asked as he turned to Bugbear.

"I don't know," Bugbear answered.

"Well, you're the one who can see in the dark, aren't you?"

"No," Bugbear said with a frown. "I'm the one who can *read* in the dark. Whatever made that noise is too far away for me to see."

Again, the moan... deep and strained, closer and more intense.

"We need a torch," Asherby insisted.

"By Oberon's satin britches," Brenen grumbled as he rummaged through his robes. He shortly produced a small globe, which he twisted, causing it to gradually glow with expanding brightness. Soon a small radius of the forest was illuminated. "Here," Brenen said, handing the globe to Asherby.

"You had that this entire time?" Asherby said, receiving the strange device.

"It's called a *will-o'-wisp*," Bugbear shrugged. "A minor contribution to the science of alchemy."

"Áes dána alchemy succeeds where goblin eyesight fails," Brenen scoffed.

"Well, technically it's based upon a Coranieid discovery," Bugbear sniffed. "As is the case with most Áes dána science. Although I'll admit, your people have added their own particular idiosyncrasies to the mystic arts."

The moan rattled their nerves once again, drawing their fear-filled eyes to the darkness. Asherby nodded to his companions and rolled the will-'o-wisp towards the unseen assailant. Slowly the area in front them was revealed, inch-by-inch and foot-by-foot, until finally stopping as it hit the tip of a leather boot. Bugbear gasped in amazement as an Áes dána warrior lumbered towards them.

"That's the same one I killed earlier!" Asherby exclaimed.

"Impossible!" Brenen balked.

"Why is he acting like that?" Bugbear said, speaking to no one but himself as he cocked his head and watched the shambling warrior with deep fascination.

"Probably because he's having a hard time breathing with that chest wound I gave him," Asherby grunted as he removed his Bowie knife from his boot.

The tall man took careful aim, throwing the knife with assassin's precision. The big blade bit deep into the warrior's skull, leaving only the hilt protruding. The warrior stumbled back a few steps, wobbled for a moment, and then lumbered forward with jagged, jerking steps.

"Nice bit of killing there," Brenen snorted.

Asherby growled at Brenen as he removed the derringer from his vest pocket. He aimed at the shambling fiend and fired. The warrior jerked as the lead ball hit its chest. But with a rattle and hiss, it continued its shuffling march towards them.

Asherby held up his stick and motioned Brenen and Bugbear behind him. "Brenen, you continue leading Bugbear to the unseelie court. I'll keep him off your trail as long as I can."

"Why don't we just run?" Brenen said, placing a hand on Asherby's shoulder. "It's very slow. Even you could probably outrun it."

"*Durm taln nawneev larnawl kir har anduv durm!*" the undead creature moaned with unearthly rage.

Bugbear's wide eyes went wide. "Of course!" he blurted as he darted towards the undead warrior.

"Bugbear!" Asherby spat, reaching out for the scurrying goblin.

But Bugbear was far too quick, and far too driven by the fuel of discovery to be halted. He stood before the undead creature who regarded the strange little man with dim, uncertain eyes.

"*Wawnur har umool,*" Bugbear hissed as he circled the warrior, dragging one foot in the dirt.

"*Durm taln nawneev larnawl kir har anduv durm!*" the creature repeated, never taking its dead eyes off of Bugbear.

"*Wawnur har umool,*" Bugbear replied, scuffing his feet into the dirt, almost as if in a ritual dance.

"*Durm taln nawneev larnawl kir har anduv durm!*" The undead warrior began to wobble as it turned, watching Bugbear's strange movements.

"*Wawnur har umool!*" Bugbear finally exclaimed, stamping his foot in the dirt before the warrior.

The creature swayed, air rattling inside its dead shell. Its mouth opened into a wide yawn, releasing soft, gray ash into the night air. Its milky eyes rolled back into its skull and it collapsed to the ground.

"What was that all about?" Asherby asked as he hobbled up to Bugbear.

"It spoke an ancient tongue," Bugbear said. "Only a handful of folk outside the dragon bride clan have ever heard it. And only two of those outsiders speak it and understand it."

"You being one of them, I presume?" Asherby said.

"Yes," Bugbear mused as he wandered away from the now inert corpse. "The other being Rígan, Brenen's predecessor."

"It spoke in Dragon?" Brenen said, looking down upon the corpse with awe.

"Yes," Bugbear answered. "It said, '*You cannot fight what is inside you.*'"

"And what was your response?" Asherby asked.

"'*There is hope.*'"

Under the glow of the will-'o-wisp, Asherby examined the markings Bugbear had made in the dirt. "And your woodland graffiti?"

"The same symbol King Martin and I used to destroy the Shadow Smith," Bugbear said as he found a suitable stone upon which to sit. He lowered his head into his hands, sighing with exhaustion. "But it doesn't make sense. Animating the dead is an unholy act. Dragons would have nothing to do with it. And yet the creature used their language."

"Makes sense to me," Asherby said, placing a boot on the side of the fallen warrior's head as he pulled his Bowie knife from its skull. "I knew some old cavalry scouts who could speak Apache as if they were born to it. Helped to know the local lingo if you ever got caught in enemy territory."

Bugbear raised an eyebrow and smiled. "That sixth grade education of yours is paying off, Asherby." Bugbear hopped off the rock and began pacing back and forth along the trail. "It was using a language it thought would help it gain trust or blend in."

"Walking around with a Bowie knife in your skull isn't the most discreet of behaviors," Asherby sniffed.

"That's the interesting bit, isn't it?" Bugbear said with upraised finger. "There was no intellect behind this. The creature was operating on pure instinct. It was as if this phrase was programmed into the very fabric of its being." Bugbear laughed and patted Asherby on the back as he ran ahead on the trail. "Come along, gentlemen!" he piped. "The sooner we get to the unseelie court, the sooner we'll have all the answers we seek!"

CHAPTER 8
THE KING'S HUNTING PARTY

Manchester secured the saddle on his purebred nektosha, a breed of horse typically only available to the dragon brides. This one was a wedding gift from Maga's sisters, and while Manchester had never been much of a horseman, he had grown quite attached to old Wahoo. Sure the horse had thrown Manchester the first few times he tried getting on. But the nektosha was a beast that rewarded persistence with loyalty. By the seventh try, Wahoo had grown accustomed to his new master's aura, and they even seemed to develop an empathic bond. Manchester was told such symbiosis between rider and nektosha was quite rare, even among the dragon brides.

Maga approached her husband, placing a hand upon his shoulder. "Loomis and his brothers are here," she whispered.

Manchester lowered his head and exhaled a long breath. He turned to see the brothers lumbering towards them through the town square, the soldiers and townsfolk who packed the wagons and horses giving the ogres wide berth.

"You be wantsing to sees us, yer majersties?" Loomis said as he smiled and bowed to the king and queen, his brothers doing likewise.

Manchester smiled weakly. He drew closer to the brothers and spoke in a hushed and secretive voice. "The queen and I are leaving town for a time. While we're gone we need you boys to do something very difficult for us."

"Naming it, boss."

"We need you to take care of the Barghest."

"Oh," Loomis laughed as he looked to his equally amused brothers. "We'll be findering the rascal!"

"No, Loomis," the king said as he lowered his eyes. "We need you to... put him down."

The ogres stopped smiling. Their faces went blank and motionless.

"He kidnapped a little girl, Loomis," Maga broke in. "He isn't a pet. He's a dangerous monster."

"Pwease to be not askering us this. We be keepering better controls over him. Big promersis."

"Promises won't keep Willow Prairie safe, boys," Manchester said, placing a comforting hand on Loomis' arm.

Loomis' eyes glistened, ringed with wet misery. "For alluva our talkering of smasherings and killerings, we never acturally been doing such a things in all our dayses."

Manchester's face fell flat with misery and guilt. "Loomis, I can ask some of the soldiers...."

"No," Loomis interrupted, taking in a deep breath and wiping the tears from his eyes. "We do what be rightly by you and Willow Prairie, boss. Barghest be our responserbility. He'll be putted down."

Manchester grimaced as the brothers turned and lumbered away. Maga placed her arms around his waist and lay her head on his shoulder.

"Do you think they'll be strong enough?" she asked.

"Yes. But it will be a while before we see them smile again."

Manchester turned to look at the people milling about the square, busily loading supplies for the expedition to Washington. Pope and a handful of his men examined their returned weapons, and loaded some of them with what little dwarven ammunition Manchester already had in his armory. Several of the Áes dána refugees also readied mounts, intent on joining the party despite Manchester's protests. About dozen of Willow Prairie's own militiamen prepared for the journey as well, assigned by Manchester to be a buffer between Pope's men and the Áes dána.

Tudmire wound his way through the crowd, his fat face a wrinkled page written with bad news. "Manchester, m'boy," he said as he approached the king and queen, "I'm afraid the journey has just become a bit more... complicated."

"How so?" Manchester sighed.

A series of shouts, cries, and expletives crackled through the town square. Riley Ratcatcher tore through the ranks, darting beneath wagons, under feet, through legs, and across paths on his way to the king and queen.

"I thought Missus Yasberry was going to watch him while we're gone," Manchester grunted to Tudmire.

"She refuses," Tudmire said with a nervous chuckle. "Seems he dug up her rose bushes, tracked mud on her Persian rug, and ate one of her chickens."

"We did not eat her chicken," Riley protested as he trotted up to them. "We only tasted it." The eager beast boy spat a feather from his mouth and wagged his tail.

"Young man," Maga started, "your antics are getting out of hand."

"Oh, we didn't go anywhere near the attic!" Riley said. "We were on the roof chasing squirrels though. And it was those squirrels that then got into the attic and did great mischief, which we're certain ol' Sour Patch Yasberry will blame on us."

"What about Sagramore?" Manchester asked Tudmire.

"He'll have his hands full watching the town while we're gone," the goblin answered. "Riley will have to come with us, I'm afraid."

"And a good thing for you," Riley said as he held up his bow and patted his quiver of arrows. "We are the best hunter in the kingdom. Every night, courtesy of our arrows, you shall dine on savory 'possum, delicious raccoon, and, if luck is with us, mouthwatering mole."

Maga groaned and turned away. "Excuse me," she gasped as she placed her hand to her mouth and staggered towards the town well.

Manchester looked after her, his brow creased with concern. He then turned sharply to Riley. "Tudmire has packed enough food to last us to Washington and back," the king said, snatching the bow from Riley. "So, you shall spend less time nocking your arrows, and more time reading your books."

Riley rolled his eyes and snorted. "Everyone wants us to read. But while we're buried in books, the kingdom will be buried in squirrels and 'possums!"

The patchwork of dog, cat, and boy padded off, his ears laid back and his tail twitching like a rattlesnake.

"He's at that age, I'm afraid," Manchester said, watching after the furry black-and-white animal boy. "Must be all the more difficult with those animal natures tugging at his leash."

"I'll keep an eye on him," Tudmire said with a reassuring pat on Manchester's hand. "Any excuse to avoid those blasted Áes dána popinjays."

Manchester chuckled. "Tudmire, you're hired."

Tudmire smiled and bowed.

A commotion near the soldiers suddenly drew their attention. Riley had a scout's coonskin cap clenched in his teeth as several of the soldiers shouted at him and tried to wrest it away.

"Looks like you have work to do," Manchester smiled to Tudmire.

Tudmire frowned as he rolled up his sleeves and charged towards the unfolding dilemma.

Manchester exhaled sharply as dusted off his top hat and placed it on his head. He then mounted Wahoo and trotted to the head of the caravan where Maga waited for him on her own nektosha. He reined his horse about and looked to the train of wagons, carts, people and animals. Save for a quick payment of gold from Tudmire to the scout with the shredded coonskin hat, the party seemed ready to head out on the trail to Washington, D.C.

"When I removed Reginald's quill from the inkwell," Manchester said to the crowd in a clear and authoritative voice, "I became the King of Willow Prairie. But that does not mean I ceased to be an American. With the great liberties this nation grants its people, comes our great responsibility to seek answers before taking action. And so, as I lead you to the nation's capital, I do so with reverence, with loyalty, with dignity. No weapon shall be raised in my name against a fellow American. No sides shall be taken in battles between government and empire. We ride in peace to speak with the President, and learn what we will of these dangerous times."

Manchester reined his horse about and leaned over to Maga. "I sounded pompous, didn't I?" he whispered.

"Like any good king should," Maga whispered with a smile.

Manchester smirked. He urged Wahoo forward as Maga and the rest of the company fell in behind him.

Tudmire grumbled as he rummaged through the utensils in his wagon. Lunch was already being prepared by his staff, and a vital cheese grater was yet missing. Without it his cigoen soufflé was certain to be a culinary disaster. Tudmire tumbled out of the wagon, tugging at his suspenders as he looked out over the temporary camp. Manchester wanted to keep on the trail until nightfall, but the Áes dána had insisted on *'Communion with the Goddess Danu'*, as they called it... some pointless ritual they seemed to trot out whenever they were of a mind to avoid or postpone something they found unpleasant. And the way they constantly groomed and fussed during the journey, Tudmire could tell the Áes dána found the dust of the trail exceedingly unpleasant.

It was when his eyes fell upon the cluster of dandies crouching together a few yards away from the chuck wagon that the mystery of his missing utensil was solved. The Áes dána were using the grater to shred a dried root into a porcelain bowl.

"Here now!" Tudmire barked as he stomped up to them. "That is the property of the Kingdom of Willow Prairie! Hand it over immediately."

The Áes dána continued grating the root, never turning about to acknowledge Tudmire. One, however, did speak to him in a haughty and dismissive tone.

"As victims of human aggression, we refuse to recognize your kingdom's claim on ownership of this device."

Tudmire fumed, his face practically boiling with rage. "Maybe you'll recognize a little goblin aggression across your silk-covered backsides, you powdered pinheads!"

Tudmire noticed a shadow falling across him. He turned about to see a rather tall and unusually broad-shouldered Áes dána standing over him, a notched arrow drawn back on his silver bow, the gleaming bodkin just inches from the goblin's fat, twitching nose.

"Before you can get to our silk-covered backsides, you'll have to get past Pfeil's arrows," the Áes dána chieftain said as he continued grating the root.

"I give you big problem, liddle gobleen," the tall archer said, his tongue thick with a foreign accent.

"Not from around here, I take it?" Tudmire said as he raised his hands.

"Part of exchange from across sea," Pfeil answered. "Arrived before worlds merged."

With a twang, buzz, and flash, Pfeil's feathered cap flew from his head, carried by an arrow to a nearby tree, where it was pinned to the trunk like a colorful bug in a schoolboy's insect collection.

"You should go back home," Riley Ratcatcher growled as he padded from the brush, notching another arrow. "And take your ugly hats with you."

Pfeil sneered at the patchwork as the other Áes dána rose from the ritual to gather about their archer. Tudmire fell back, a triumphant smile on his face as he placed a hand upon Riley's shoulder.

"Now then," the goblin said, "I shall ask you again to please return my cheese grater."

"Your pet does not intimidate us," the chieftain snorted. "He took Pfeil by surprise once. But by the time he could get off another arrow, our champion would have emptied his quiver into the creature's heart."

"Oh?" Tudmire said with a voice dripping in sarcasm. "Your obelisk is a champion archer, is he?"

"I once hit pea off tip uf man's tongue," Pfeil boasted with a shrug and smirk.

"So you missed his tongue?" Riley laughed.

Pfeil stepped towards Riley, his face pulled into a scowl. "You liddle dog! What do you know of true bogenschiessen?"

"We never miss," Riley snarled as he stepped towards Pfeil. "That is all we need to know. And that is all you need to know."

Pfeil held up a small gold medallion that hung about his neck on a thin silver chain. "See this? I win in bogenschiessen tournament. My bogenschiessen is best."

Tudmire stepped between the two archers, his brain percolating like a coffee pot full of devious ideas. "Perhaps a little contest is in order?" he said with an arched brow.

"What do you have in mind?" the Áes dána chieftain asked, his voice laced with interest.

Tudmire stroked all three of his chins in severe thought. As his eyes absently grazed through the treetops the distant honking of a flock of geese broke over the horizon. Suddenly an idea struck him. "Each archer gets a single arrow," he said with upraised finger. "The one to knock down the most apples from yonder apple tree wins."

"Is simple," Pfeil said as he stepped forward, drawing an arrow from his quiver.

Tudmire raised a hand to stop the big Áes dána. "Hold on a moment. Let's make the contest... interesting."

"How so?" the chieftain said.

"If Pfeil wins, you keep the cheese grater, and I'll be your butler for the remainder of the journey."

"And if your animal wins?"

"If my *good and noble friend*, Riley wins," Tudmire said with a sour smirk, "you return the cheese grater and keep your annoying traps shut until we get to Washington."

"Is deal," Pfeil laughed. "I go first."

The Áes dána archer stepped forward, his narrow eyes scanning the tree tops, picking out an area with the largest concentration of apples. He let fly with his arrow. The missile sped into the leafy canopy, piercing leaves and fruit. By the time the arrow punched into a tree trunk it had pierced three apples, and knocked another six to the ground.

"Nine apples," the chieftain said. "Let's see your *good and noble friend* beat that."

Riley frowned as he nocked his arrow on the bowstring. "You should not have put so much confidence in us, Turdmore," the beast boy whispered to the goblin. "The queen has not had time to practice with us of late."

Tudmire smiled as he patted the boy on the shoulder. "Don't let those bullies intimidate you, m'boy. Remember, what's bad for the goose is good for the gambler." The goblin winked to Riley.

Riley cocked his head with confusion. Then as he heard the honking overhead, a slow, canny smile crept along his muzzle. Riley quickly raised his bow, aiming his arrow straight into the air. The shaft flew true, high into the sky, above the treetops and out of sight.

The cluster of Áes dána dandies laughed.

"Your bogenschiessen is weak," Pfeil spat at Riley.

"We prefer tea precisely at 9, noon, and 3," the chieftain sniffed to Tudmire. "And we expect our robes washed and pressed by...."

Tudmire held up a finger as he listened, his big ear turned skyward. There was a distant rush of air, as if something was falling towards the clearing. Suddenly, a dead goose crashed through the branches, Riley's arrow sticking in its chest. It fell at Tudmire's feet like a burlap sack full of wet cheese.

The Áes dána looked at the dead goose with alarm. And their alarm grew ten-fold as roughly twenty apples came drip-drop-kerplopping down upon their heads.

"Oooohhh!" Tudmire exclaimed as he licked his lips and rubbed his hands. He plucked the goose up by its neck. "Tonight for supper we'll have roasted goose with apple stuffing." The goblin sauntered up to the chieftain, holding out his hand. "I'll need my grater."

The chieftain grumbled as he placed the utensil in the goblin's hand. "Most unfair."

"Ah ah ah," Tudmire said with a shaking head. "A deal is a deal. No more talking."

The Áes dána clenched his teeth and pressed his lips together until they became a thin line of frustration. With a rustle of purple cloaks, the company of coxcombs stormed back to their wagon to stew and pout over their defeat.

Pfeil hesitated, regarding Riley with cold, hard eyes. Then with a small, begrudging smile, he nodded to the beast boy, turned, and joined the others.

Tudmire walked up to Riley, his face about four-fifths smile. "Best wager I ever made, dear boy."

"You didn't even win any money," Riley said as he pulled his arrow from the goose's gullet.

Tudmire took a victorious bite out of one of the apples. "Áes dána silver is fine," he said, spitting bits of apple and juice. "But Áes dána silence is golden."

"Áes dána silver is fine, but Áes dána silence is golden."

CHAPTER 10

ON THE EDGE OF UNSEELIE

Bugbear stirred the smoldering embers of the small campfire. Asherby and Brenen yet slept, squeezing in the few hours of rest Bugbear had allowed them. The goblin turned back to the book he had been studying... the mysterious tome filled with notes Bugbear had written to himself, but which Bugbear never remembered writing.

One particular passage stood out, circled in red ink with stars and exclamation points scribbled about it. *"During the cataclysm, the draugen were cast into the other world,"* Bugbear read aloud. Notes were scrawled next to the passage. *"Saint George. Plagues. The enemy within."*

Bugbear closed the book with frustration. "Couldn't you have simply given me a straight answer, Bugbear?" he hissed to himself. "Now I know how Manchester must feel." He sighed as he threw the stick into the ashes of the fire. "I really am a hateful little twit."

Asherby roused, wincing as he moved his leg. He gently propped himself up against a log and yawned as he nodded to Bugbear. "Couldn't sleep?"

"I don't sleep much these days," Bugbear answered. The goblin stood up and paced about the clearing. "Too much to do. Too much to learn. No rest for the witty."

Asherby looked up into the sky, squinting his eyes against the brightness of the afternoon sun. "What time is it? Three? Four?"

Bugbear fumbled with his gold pocket watch, a gift from the king and queen. A decorative bee adorned on the outside, and on the inside was the inscription: *"There are four basic precepts of Non-Logical Thought, which can never be repeated enough. Number one: Reality is Thought. Number two: Logic restricts Thought and thus restricts Reality. Number three: Abandon Logic..."* And apparently the engraver had run out of room halfway through the third precept. But, much as with Non-Logic itself, it was the thought that counted.

"3:34 p.m. precisely," Bugbear reported as he flipped the watch closed. "Well past the deadline I gave you and Brenen for hitting the trail again."

Asherby took up his banderberry cane and nudged the snoring Brenen. Brenen waved him off. "Wake up, your majesty," Asherby said, poking the Áes dána king again. And again Brenen snorted and waved his tormenter away.

"Oh, for the love of hate!" Bugbear spat. He stormed over to the campfire, dipping the tip of his shoe into the embers and flicking a coal towards Brenen.

The coal rolled into the drowsing dandy's robes, smoldering for a few moments before igniting the fibers. Brenen bolted awake as the flames began to creep up his garments. His eyes bloated with panic, he rolled and floundered in the dirt as he tore the robes from his body. Brenen then rolled to his feet, stomping on the smoldering clothing and kicking dirt over it.

"You're responsible for this!" Brenen panted and wheezed as he turned to Bugbear.

"Certainly," Bugbear replied.

"Are you insane?" Brenen raged.

"Well, yes," Bugbear said with a shrug. "I thought we had already pretty much established that." The goblin turned to Asherby for confirmation. "Hadn't we already established that?"

"Yes," Asherby replied with a nod. "It is common knowledge."

Brenen frowned as he plucked the charred robe from the dirt. "This was a gift from my cousin, Corcra."

"You should have taken better care of it," Bugbear said as he took up his book and waddled towards the trail.

Asherby patted Brenen on the shoulder. "Too hot to wear a robe anyway," he smiled as he hobbled after Bugbear.

"When the robe is on fire, yes," Brenen grunted as he threw the ruined garment to the ground. He stormed after Asherby and Bugbear, fumbling about his breeches and tunic for pockets in which to place his hands.

"This cousin of yours," Asherby asked Brenen as the king caught up to them, "he royalty like you?"

"He is head of a Hibernian clan overseas," Brenen said with a nod. "Very skilled harpist and poet."

"Ah," Asherby said with interest. "So you Áes dána have kin in other parts of the world? Interesting. I myself have quite a diverse background. My father was half Irish and half Cherokee. And my mother's side of the family is Lebanese by way of Mexico."

"An excellent pedigree, Asherby," Bugbear noted. "As varied and colorful as the country you serve."

"And that is my dream, Bugbear," Asherby said, his eyes absently going skyward. "Someday when I settle down with the right woman, our children will have ancestors whose stories stretch back to the dawn of time and across all four corners of the globe. They'll be as American as the mountains, and rivers, and forests around them. But in their veins will flow the promise of a better world."

Brenen snorted scornfully. "Hopefully the promise of better metaphors as well."

"That was a bit... flowery," Bugbear said with a chortle. "Even for a human."

Asherby smiled and lowered his head sheepishly. "I'm sorry for the digression, gentlemen. I'll keep my Quixotic dreams to myself in the future."

Bugbear smiled reassuringly to Asherby. "Noble dreams they are, my friend. Don't be ashamed in sharing them."

Brenen sighed with impatience. "Can we drop all of these false pleasantries?" he asked. "This talk of different cultures and races all getting along... foolishness. As long as there are people, there will be wars. There will be strife. And dreams, noble and otherwise, will be shattered."

Bugbear stopped, turning to Brenen with his face wrinkled in irritation. "I simply must know," the goblin started, "do you wake up in the morning and say to yourself *'How many stupid things can I fit into this day? What phenomenally stupid acts can I perform? What embarrassingly stupid words can I utter?'* Is that how you start your day? Or does the stupidity just flow naturally through your being? Is it like breathing? Or do you have to concentrate to be so stupid?"

Brenen backed away, sputtering and fuming like a lit fuse.

"You know," Bugbear continued, "if they were to gather all of the stupid people in the world in one place and hold a competition to see which one was the stupidest, I imagine you'd lose. Simply because you'd be too stupid to find your way. And even if you did happen to get there, it would be on the wrong day. That is how utterly and completely stupid you are."

"Are you quite finished insulting me?" Brenen asked, finally finding his voice.

"Are you quite finished being stupid?" Bugbear answered, poking the nobleman in the chest.

Asherby hobbled between the two. "Kind of making Brenen's point here about folks not getting along, aren't you, Bugbear?"

The goblin raised his eyebrows, his anger being replaced by

awareness. He shook his head and looked to the ground. "My apologies, Brenen. I fear I overreacted."

Brenen grumbled and grunted. "That's okay."

Bugbear smiled and nodded. "And I shouldn't have burned your robe."

Brenen waved his hand. "Don't worry about it."

"And I shouldn't have used your toothbrush to scrub the fungus between my toes."

"That's al.... What?"

Bugbear fumbled about in his waistcoat, finally finding the implement and handing it over to Brenen. "Those pig bristles really don't stand up to much punishment. Got to the middle toe on my left foot before the last one fell out."

Brenen looked at the ivory-handled brush, now stripped of its bristles and caked with globs of green fungus and mucous.

"Now dwarves," Bugbear said with a chuckle as he turned about, "they make sturdy toothbrushes. Might want to look into that."

"I'll wring his fat little neck," Brenen hissed as he tossed the despoiled toothbrush to the ground.

"Don't be stupid," Asherby winked as he hobbled past.

Bugbear stopped some ten feet up the trail. To the side stood a tree, its thick trunk tattooed with strange symbols, carved deep into the wood and stained with dyes and paints. "Brenen," Bugbear called back. "Didn't you say we were another day's walk from the unseelie court?"

"Yes," Brenen grumbled as he came up behind Bugbear. "At least."

"Then correct me if I'm wrong, but is this not an unseelie mark?" Bugbear asked as he ran his fingers along the deep carving.

Brenen peered at the marking, his face lighting with surprise.

"Yes, it is. Not a forgery or imitation either. It was carved by an Áes dána blade."

"This is a bad sign," Bugbear said with a heavy sigh.

"Why?" Asherby asked as he limped up to them. "We just shaved a day off our journey."

"Yes," Bugbear said. "But that's only because the unseelie court has expanded its territory. And that means something or someone has been throwing rocks at their hive."

"You think someone is trying to draw them into the conflict between us and the Áes dána?" Asherby asked.

"Not only have they tried," a voice growled from behind them, "but they have succeeded."

Bugbear, Brenen, and Asherby turned about to see a pack of six Áes dána warriors surrounding them. Each had some manner of wound or deformity, and each held either a bow, a gun, or a blade. Their armor and colors were much less uniform than the typical Áes dána warrior, and they held themselves in a much rougher and more practical manner.

"Oh," Bugbear said with a smile, "very sneaky, this lot. Didn't even hear a twig snap." Bugbear looked to Brenen and Asherby. "Did either of you hear them?"

Brenen and Asherby shook their heads as they raised their hands in surrender.

"Ah, yes," Bugbear said as he imitated his comrades. "The raising of hands. Must observe the rituals."

"Why are you in unseelie territory?" a broad-shouldered warrior with an eyepatch asked.

"A better question is, why is unseelie territory surrounding us?" Bugbear said.

"We have been forced to expand due to Áes dána raids on our

holdings," the warrior spat. "Our limited resources have been confiscated for *the war effort*."

"Well, we may be able to put an end to all of this," Bugbear said. "If you'll simply allow me access to your library."

The warrior laughed. "We've already caught one of your kind trying to sneak off with our sacred writings, goblin. We may be unseelie, but we aren't stupid. You won't be allowed anywhere near our library."

"Wait!" Bugbear blurted. "Another goblin was seeking something in your library?"

"Yes. Caught him there a night ago."

"May I speak with him?" Bugbear asked, his voice sharpened with anxiety.

"Perhaps," the warrior said as he motioned his men to gather the prisoners. "That will be up to Queen Rígan. Take them to Dun Feasa."

The motley pack of warriors herded Bugbear, Brenen, and Asherby down the trail. Bugbear studied the unseelie warriors closely, for in all his travels he had never encountered their kind before. The goblin noticed they carried a hodgepodge of weapons and equipment. Much of their arsenal was standard Áes dána issue, although a bit more used and worse-for-wear. But they also carried some human items, such as guns, knives, and watches. Their uniforms were tattered and stained with blood from past battles, and some holes were patched with animal skins or leather scraps. They were mostly unshaven, which was unheard of in proper Áes dána society. Their hair either grew loose and wild like the thick briars and bramble of the forest, or it was pulled back into ponytails, topknots, or some other simple style. In all, the appearance of the unseelie made for a stark contrast to Brenen's fine silk garments and impeccable grooming.

Brenen's face dripped with worry, his feet dragging along the forest floor like prison chains. "Rígan," he whispered.

Bugbear looked to Brenen with a smile. "Maybe she won't recognize you with the bandages," the goblin whispered.

Brenen's mood lightened slightly. "Do you suppose?"

"And the robe," Asherby added quietly. "You'll be just another commoner to her without that fancy robe."

Brenen nodded and smiled. "You're right! She'll never know I'm a king!"

Upon hearing the outburst, the unseelie band turned to glare at Brenen. Bugbear winced, ducking his head down into his shoulders. Asherby shook his head and sighed.

The one-eyed warrior marched up to Brenen. He looked the king over and smiled as recognition widened his one good eye. "So, it's you, Brenen?" he grunted. "The Queen will be especially pleased to take an audience with you. Make no mistake of that." The warrior grabbed Brenen by the back of the neck and shoved him forward.

The disgraced Áes dána king staggered, his head now heavy with certain doom. Bugbear and Asherby walked beside him, the unseelie guards continuing to march them along the forest trail.

"Have I told you lately how stupid you are?" Bugbear finally asked Brenen.

CHAPTER 11
THE 3:10 FROM TOLEDO

Manchester reined his horse to a stop. He looked down the long stitch of train tracks that wound eastward. In the distance he saw dark, still shapes scattered across the tracks, obscured in the shadows cast by the setting sun.

"What is it?" Maga asked as she rode up beside him.

"The 3:10 from Toledo," Manchester replied.

He reined Wahoo about and trotted back to the company. He waved to Tudmire, who waddled off of his driver's seat on the chuck wagon and scurried over. "Set up camp here for the night," Manchester ordered. "Make sure everyone stays put. The queen and I are going to scout the surrounding area."

Tudmire saluted and smiled. "We'll have the tents pitched and the campfires lit by the time you return. Although supper may be a bit late. Someone's wandered off with my pepper."

Manchester fidgeted in his saddle, fingering the container of pepper hidden in his vest pocket. He had felt slightly guilty in secretly snatching it from Tudmire's chuck wagon, but as good as the goblin's cooking was, he had yet to control his tendencies to use too much pepper. "Uhm," Manchester started, "why don't you try cooking with some different spices tonight. I hear turmeric is quite healthy."

"Not a bad idea," Tudmire said with a nod. He then scurried off to make preparations for the camp.

Manchester road back to Maga at the train tracks, only to find Pope there, grinning as his teeth ground on a wad of chewing tobacco.

"That's a nasty habit," Manchester scowled.

"Finest chaw in Boston," Pope drawled.

"I was talking about leaving formation without my permission," Manchester replied with a sardonic grin. "But since you're here, you can keep a lookout while Maga and I examine the train wreck."

"Better than listening to your goblin's camp songs," Pope said with a tip of his hat.

Manchester puckered his brow as he urged Wahoo into a canter down the tracks. Maga and Pope fell in behind him.

Horse hooves on loose gravel. The faint smell of coal. The thickening shadows of sunset. And a thin trickle of trepidation. These were the sensations that met Manchester as they rode up to the hollow husk of the 3:10 from Toledo. Manchester drew his pistol as they approached to the wreck, nodding to Maga and Pope to ready their weapons as well. Maga drew her sword and Pope unsheathed his rifle.

Manchester pulled Wahoo to a stop a few yards from the overturned boxcars. A sliver of shadow darted between the cars, followed by a scuffle, metallic clank, and a string of gruff curses.

"Come out!" Manchester shouted, leveling his pistol in the direction of the commotion.

"Come again?" a gravel voice replied.

"I said, come out!" Manchester repeated.

"What did he say?" the voice growled, seemingly speaking to someone other than Manchester.

"Hold up!" another, softer voice called out from the wreckage. "They want us to come out," the softer voice said in a lower tone.

"Why should we?" the gravel voice complained.

Manchester frowned and stirred in his saddle. He grunted as he fired his pistol into the air. "Because the gun is asking you nicely."

"They have guns," the softer voice said with worry.

"I know!" the gravel voice blurted. "I ain't completely deaf!"

"We're coming out!" the softer voice called. "Don't shoot!"

There was some fumbling and a bit more cursing before a tall, lanky youth and a stout, sooty dwarf stumbled out into the waning twilight.

Manchester squinted and waved the pair closer with his pistol. "We won't shoot," Manchester promised. "Just want a few answers."

The youth and dwarf cautiously approached. As they drew closer, Manchester could see that both of them wore packs loaded with various tools, pieces of scrap metal, and other odds and ends. Both seemed quite travel-worn as well, covered in dirt and burs, with a few bruises and small cuts thrown in. They stopped a few feet from Manchester, Maga, and Pope, their hands raised in surrender.

"What are you two doing rummaging about in a train wreck?" Manchester asked.

"Just came upon it," the youth said, lifting the aviator goggles from his eyes to rest on his forehead. "Thought we'd check for survivors."

"Ain't none," the dwarf added. "No bodies neither."

"Could've been eaten by coyotes," Pope offered.

"Nope," the youth said. "We seen some animal tracks, but they was leading way from the train."

"There were circus animals on that train, Martin," Maga said. "I remember Riley was quite excited about it."

"We don't have time to round them up now," Manchester said. "Been three days since she derailed anyway. No telling where those animals have gotten to." Manchester turned back to the youth and the dwarf. "So where do you two hail from?"

"Out west," the youth answered. "Place called Chugwater. My name's Bixby and this here is Cobblestone."

"Shush, boy!" the dwarf said with a nudge to the young man's ribs. "Ain't no call to tell no more than what's been asked of you."

Pope nudged Manchester and pointed to the strange copper *hammer and lightning* pins that adorned the collars of Bixby and Cobblestone. "I know that symbol," he said. "Belongs to a new kind of cult that's sprung up lately. My men and I ran into a few of them, raiding abandoned copper mines."

"Ain't no cult!" Bixby protested. "We're Dabblers!"

"Blast it, boy!" Cobblestone exclaimed, throwing his bowler to the ground. "You can't go givin' away lodge secrets like that!"

Maga leaned over to whisper to Manchester. "My sisters have come across their type as well. Humans and dwarves. Some kind of joint venture in engineering and invention. Mostly harmless, and possibly useful."

Manchester nodded and smiled to his wife. "Well, Bixby and Cobblestone," Manchester started as he turned to the Dabblers, "it's getting too dark to examine the wreckage now. We'll leave it till the morning. In the meantime, you're more than welcome to clean up and have a bite to eat at our camp."

"Gosh, Mister," Bixby said as he pulled his stocking hat and goggles from his head and wrung them in his hands, "we ain't had a proper meal in I don't know how long."

"Or a bath," Cobblestone added, plugging his nose and looking to Bixby with distaste. "You humans stir up an awful funk when you travel."

Manchester smiled as he holstered his pistol and reined Wahoo about. "Follow us, gentlemen. I believe roasted goose with apple stuffing is on the menu for tonight."

CHAPTER 12
SPEAKING WITH THE DEAD

Bugbear, Asherby, and Brenen were shoved to their knees before Queen Rígan's throne. The throne room itself was a mix of majestic and organic, being composed mostly of a wide circle of stone monoliths covered in thick carpets of green vines. The roof of the room was open, and the moon and stars held court overhead even as Rígan held court below. She gazed down from her throne of twisted oak roots cushioned with patches of gray moss. Save for her missing right arm, she was as perfect and beautiful as any queen could expect to be. Clear porcelain skin, rich red curls, deep ocean-blue eyes, lips curved thick like rose petals. If not for the way she turned and fidgeted in her seat, one would have thought she was a statue carved by a master sculptor. Only the tattered purple gown she wore and the tarnished crown upon her brow dimmed her goddess light and dragged her down to the level of mere mortals.

"What visitors have you brought me at this late hour, Threelgon?" Rígan asked, gazing down upon the prisoners with amusement.

"We caught them by our new borders to the north," the one-eyed warrior answered. "Seeing as how we've recently had problems with goblin sneak-thieves, I thought it best to bring them here for questioning."

"Your majesty," Bugbear began as he pulled himself to his feet, "it really is very imperative that I..."

"It is imperative that you do not speak unless spoken to, goblin," Rígan sneered.

"Listen, lady," Asherby said, groaning as he stood to address the queen, "you need to hear him out."

"And should I listen to you as well? A man who serves in the army of this foolish American nation?"

"Well, ma'am," Asherby nodded, "I suppose my country may seem a bit more foolish than most, if only because we allow our fools to speak freely."

Rígan's mouth curved to a begrudging smile. She leaned back on her throne and motioned to Bugbear. "Then speak, fool."

Bugbear gave Asherby a narrow-eyed glance as he shook his head. "Queen Rígan, it has come to my attention that you may have vital information in your library."

"And how has this come to your attention?" the queen asked.

Bugbear hesitated, his mouth twitching as though trying to decide which words to release and which words to keep captive. "I read it in a book."

"Which book?"

"That isn't important," Bugbear grumbled as he ran his hands through his tangled mop of hair.

"It's a book in which he wrote notes he hasn't written yet," Asherby said matter-of-factly.

"What did you say?" Rígan asked as she moved forward, brows arched in alarm.

"It's complicated," Bugbear said, holding his hands up to the queen. "But my theory is that somehow something I've written in the future has found it's way to me in the present."

"Come with me," she said, rising from the throne and walking to the archway. She motioned to the guards to gather the prisoners and follow.

They walked upon meandering footpaths cut through the unseelie camp. Occasionally a soot-faced soul would glance up with bitter suspicion as the prisoners passed their little clusters of campfires. Asherby tried to smile to them, while Bugbear returned their glares with google-eyed annoyance. Brenen, however, kept his head down and his gaze to the trail.

Shortly, Rígan and her guards brought the captives to a large black boulder set upon a small flat-topped hill. Dimly, in the thin moonlight, Bugbear could see a stunted, shadowed shape chained to the rock. Wide, milky eyes blinked in the darkness, watching the guards as they approached with guns and swords drawn. The heavy chains rattled slightly as the figure shifted and strained. And then with a thin, cutting voice it spoke: *"Hulth mulnjan mustak likhar anduv marzul."*

Bugbear shivered, the voice trickling through his ears and into his brain, where it seized his nerves like a cold claw from the grave. *"The hand from the future writes in the past,"* he gasped.

"Ah," Rígan said. "You understand Dragon Speak?"

"Yes," Bugbear replied with a shudder.

"Then you would be Bugbear, advisor to King Martin of Willow Prairie?"

"I am," Bugbear said, his composure slowly returning.

Rígan motioned to the shadowy form chained to the rock. "I had thought perhaps this creature was you, given its familiarity with such a rare language. But, considering its... condition, I had my doubts."

"It's condition?" Bugbear said with arched brow.

Rígan nodded to Threelgon. The tall warrior removed a will-o'-wisp from his tunic, giving it a quick twist. Soon the hilltop was aglow with the arcane light. The creature chained to the rock, hissed and shied from the light, straining at the chains in an attempt to escape. Bugbear's eyes bulged with recognition. It was a goblin... a sick goblin, with gray skin stretched over a skeletal frame, teeth sharpened to points, and eyes white and lifeless. And to the side, out of reach with tip buried into the earth, stuck the shovel the creature had once carried in life.

"Duergar," Bugbear breathed.

Duergar turned to Bugbear upon hearing his name. The dull and lifeless eyes seemed to suddenly gleam with demonic intellect. Duergar cocked his head, the vertebrae in his neck cracking with a sickening music. He smiled as his tongue rolled out, licking dull fangs. *"Hulth mulnjan mustak likhar anduv marzul."*

"Why do you get to come back?" Bugbear suddenly growled. The stunted scholar darted like a ball of lightning to the shovel. He pulled it from the dirt and bolted over to Duergar. With a rage that boiled from the center of his soul to the edge of his being, Bugbear laid the shovel aside Duergar's head. The undead gardener laughed as the blow sent his melon head wobbling on his cornstalk neck. "All those people in Willow Prairie!" Bugbear bashed the other side of Duergar's head. "Mother Twitchett!" Bugbear brought the shovel down around on top of Duergar's flat head. "All dead! But *you* get to come back!"

It was some moments before the startled unseelie guards gathered the wits and the courage to restrain Bugbear. They tore the shovel from his hands, throwing it to the ground. Bugbear tugged and pulled against them. "Let me go!" he demanded. "I'm not done being indignant yet!"

"Calm your companion, sir!" Rígan urged Asherby.

"I thought he had things well in hand," Asherby shrugged.

Duergar laughed, licking the black blood from his lips as his wobbling head turned to the gathering. "You think you're ready for war," he hissed, "yet you have no idea the enemy you face."

"Who?" Bugbear yelled as he slipped out of his coat and escaped his unseelie captors. "Who?" he snarled as he approached Duergar.

"Durm taln nawneev larnawl kir har anduv durm," Duergar

chanted. *"You cannot fight what is inside you.* You cannot fight the Baymaari."

With a demented cackle, Duergar burst his chains, diving onto Bugbear with both hands on the scholar's throat. Bugbear gasped and wheezed as the black-nailed fingers dug deep into his windpipe. Threelgon plunged his blade into Duergar's side, but the undead goblin kept choking his erstwhile friend, his white eyes framed in delirious glee. Remembering Manchester's similar encounter with Duergar the year before, Bugbear pulled his pocket watch from his vestments and slapped it into the side of his attacker's head. Duergar's flesh crackled like frying bacon and his mouth pulled into a tortured moan. The undead gardener bolted from Bugbear, bowling over the unseelie warriors. He darted down the hillside and into the forest, disappearing like a fog on the wind. Rígan motioned and Threelgon and several of his warriors dashed down the hill in pursuit.

"They'll never catch him," Bugbear coughed as he sat up. "The only reason he allowed himself to be captured in the first place was because he knew I was coming."

Asherby quickly helped Bugbear to his feet. "What was that all about?" the tall man asked, gazing out across the dark landscape of the night-shrouded forest.

Bugbear rubbed his neck, gasping and wheezing for breath. "Duergar," the goblin said after several deep breaths. "A lifetime ago, he was a friend of mine. But he fell under the thrall of the Shadow Smith. He was killed at the Battle of Tamarack last year."

"And yet here he is, back from the dead," Asherby said. "Just like the Áes dána soldier who attacked us earlier. But how?"

"The Baymaari," Rígan said in a low voice.

"What's that?" Asherby asked.

"In Dragon Speak," Bugbear shuddered, "it means *Plague.*"

CHAPTER 13
A NIGHT AT THE CIRCUS

Manchester walked over to the campfire after getting himself a second helping of Tudmire's roasted goose. He squatted on a rock next to Maga. As he chewed on the succulent meat he looked to Maga and raised his plate to her in offering.

Maga covered her mouth and turned away. "Not hungry," she whispered.

Manchester shrugged and continued eating. Across from him sat Pope and one of his men, along with the two Dabblers they had recently picked up. The Dabblers were a tad cleaner after washing up at a nearby spring, but they yet wore the same tattered clothes and carried the same packs overflowing with pieces of metal and machinery.

A few yards in the distance in the light of a will-o'-wisp, Riley practiced his archery under the guidance of Pfeil. Apparently, Tudmire had allowed an exception to his wager with the Áes dána refugees. Manchester was not too upset by the deviation in Riley's studies, as earlier in the day on the trail ride the boy had worked through quite a few complex ciphers and recited all 45 state capitals. Although, Manchester was beginning to wonder how accurate that information would be any more. There was obviously some power yet being exerted by the federal government, but how far this stable influence reached throughout the country Manchester had no idea.

Tudmire came over and sat beside the king, his own plate piled with steaming goose meat and apple stuffing. The goblin inhaled and sighed. "You were right about that turmeric, m'boy," he smiled. "So, Manchester tells me you two are inventors," Tudmire said to the Dabblers between mouthfuls of goose. "What exactly have you invented?"

"Nothing yet," Bixby answered enthusiastically. "But we're working on a mechanical lady."

"Stop giving away our secrets, boy!" Cobblestone blurted as he elbowed the youth, spilling his stuffing on the ground.

"What secrets?" Bixby said as he plucked the stuffing off the ground and plopped it into his mouth. "You got a big mechanical leg sticking out of your pack." Bixby grabbed the metal foot and waved it at Cobblestone. *"Hello? Remember me?"*

"Why a lady and not a man?" Pope chuckled.

"He's afraid a man might beat him up," Cobblestone scoffed.

"Ain't so!" Bixby said. "I just never known a woman to be mean, that's all."

"Ha!" Tudmire laughed. "You haven't met my Aunt Winkle!"

Maga turned to Bixby, the discomfort of earlier suddenly melting away. "You can't be more than 14 years old, lad. How many women have you even met?"

"Most of the women I knew was killed," Bixby replied, his eyes turning to the fire. "My ma, all her friends. Killed in a hotel fire set by men who thought folks hadn't ought to live a certain way."

"Awww," Cobblestone said with a shake of his head, "now ye got him started agin."

"I'm sorry," Maga said, her face suddenly flush with embarrassment. "I was only curious." She stood and briskly strode away from the fire, towards her horse near the edge of camp.

"Now you got her started again," Manchester said with a sour smirk to Cobblestone. He dumped his remaining goose meat onto Tudmire's plate before rising to join his wife.

"Don't tell me," Maga said as she noticed Manchester coming up behind her. "I'm acting strangely again, right?"

"Not really," Manchester said, placing a hand on her shoulder.

"The dwarf is a little jackass. I was ready to leave too."

Maga offered a weak smile as she kissed his hand. "Another orphan on our doorstep, Martin," she said, turning to brush her horse's mane. "What is it about this world that makes parents such an endangered species?"

"Not endangered," Manchester replied. "Just valuable."

Maga turned away, her eyes falling on Riley and Pfeil in the distance, the eerie light of the will-o'-wisp illuminating their nocturnal archery practice. She exhaled sharply as she turned back to Manchester. "He's been through so much the past year. Losing Mother Twitchett. What Cron did to him. The battle at Tamarack. We're supposed to be looking after him. We're supposed to be his guardians." She looked to the ground, her silver eyes dimmed by guilt and regret. "But we've been passing him off to Missus Yasberry, Tudmire, and now this Áes dána stranger. Riley deserves better guardians."

Manchester nodded, his lips pulled into a sour frown. "He deserves... parents."

Some great animal bellowed in the night, rattling the timbers of the forest. Manchester and Maga both looked off to the distance, watching the trees tremble and splinter before some unseen force.

"My wife lost her nose," Manchester gasped.

"What?" Maga said, with a sideways glance and crinkled brow.

"Never mind," Manchester said, shaking his head and huffing his breath.

And by *"Never mind"* Manchester really meant *"I don't have time to explain some mostly trivial experience in my past that for some reason has stayed with me all of these years as an odd phrase I instinctively blurt out at inappropriate times."*

For you see, when Manchester was a boy his father had taken him to a vaudeville show at the Tibbits Theater in Branch County. In between the jugglers and musicians, a comedy team had performed a doctor skit in which a man's wife had lost her nose.

"How does she smell?" the doctor had asked.

"Awful," the husband had replied.

Manchester was so delighted by the joke that he told, re-told, and re-re-told it at every family gathering thereafter. He told it so often that as he grew older he would sometimes find himself saying, "My wife lost her nose," whenever he got into a situation that had a bad *smell* about it. While those around him often expressed confusion at such a seemingly random and unusual proclamation, to Manchester it was simply another way of saying "Oh... poop."

Manchester bolted towards the other side of camp. Maga grabbed her bow and quiver and followed.

"King Munchausen!" Riley shouted excitedly as he ran towards them. "We're sorry!"

"What did you do?" Manchester asked as he stopped and peered into the gloom of the forest beyond.

"Was my fault," Pfeil said. "Was teaching boy trick shot when will-o'-wisp went out. He get confused and miss his mark."

"But what did he hit?" Manchester asked.

The beast continued to thunder its pain and rage, stomping closer and closer to the camp.

"Everyone back!" Manchester commanded as he drew his pistols.

Maga readied her bow, as Pfeil pulled Riley back to join the Áes dána. Pope kept just behind Manchester and Maga, his men ready with rifles and pistols.

The ground shook, and a deep, heavy breathing boiled from the forest. It drew closer, closer, and closer. Until finally it stopped.

"Is it gone?" Tudmire asked, stepping towards the king. His foot hit the unlit will-o'-wisp, sending it rolling across the camp and towards the forest. The device suddenly sputtered to life, sending its amber glow up into the face of a huge beast, at least twice the size of the biggest ogre. It's maw was ringed with razor teeth, and curved ivory tusks jutted from its jaws. The beast's long trunk raised in the air as it released a terrible trumpet of agony. It shook its thick mane of fur, feline eyes glaring at the tiny creatures cowering before it.

Manchester saw its thick, round foot stamping in the dirt, blood seeping between two of its clawed toes. The crack of gunfire suddenly broke the night as one of Pope's men let nerves get the better of him. Manchester cursed as he saw the creature's eyes light with rage. It charged out of the forest and into the camp. The rest of Pope's men opened fire with their weapons, most of which seemed to have no effect. Maga launched an arrow, which bounced off the creature's thick, gray hide. But Manchester stood his ground as the monster stormed towards him. As it bent down to gorge him with its tusks, the king grabbed the ivory tip and swung himself up and over onto its head.

"Hold your fire!" Maga commanded. "You'll hit the king!"

The company scattered as the beast continued its charge, Manchester holding onto great handfuls of fur as he rode upon its head. As the trunk twined up to grasp him, Manchester felt the tingle of inspiration. He reached into his vest pocket, removing the container of pepper he had taken from Tudmire earlier in the day. As the trunk opening came towards him, Manchester emptied the entire contents of the container. In the ensuing chaos, Manchester lost his grip on the mane and tumbled to the forest floor. He barely escaped the thunderous feet of the creature as it staggered and wheezed. The king watched its tree trunk foot slam down onto his top hat, which fortunately no longer covered his head. Maga darted towards Manchester, dragging him to safety. Both of them watched from the brush as the massive animal groaned and gasped, tripping towards the forest in confusion. Its trunk stretched out, trembling and quivering like a water moccasin, until finally issuing a trumpeting sneeze. It staggered into the forest, where it unleashed several more of the rumbling expulsions, until its rampage faded slowly into the night.

The travelers gathered at the edge of camp and looked off into the nighttime forest.

"That would account for at least two of our circus animals," Manchester observed as he struggled to his feet with Maga's help.

"But how?" Maga asked. "Cron has been dead for months. Only she could have created more patchworks."

"Let's follow it and find out," Manchester shrugged. He hobbled over to the path of destruction, picking up his flattened hat. He popped it back into shape, but scowled as he poked a finger through the seem at the top. "Pope, you bring two of your men. Pfeil, you're welcome to join us as well."

"And us?" Riley said as he trotted up to Manchester.

"Too dangerous, son," Manchester said as he patted the disappointed patchwork's head. "Stay here and help Tudmire watch the camp."

"But it was our fault," Riley protested. "We should…"

Pfeil placed a hand on Riley's shoulder. "I count on you to stay and protect my friends wid your bogenschiessen. Okay? You do that for Pfeil?"

"Okay," Riley grumbled.

"You good friend," Pfeil said, playfully ruffling Riley's hair.

Manchester looked to Maga. " You're the only one of us who can see in the dark. You best take the lead."

Maga nodded as she moved into the brush, the others filing in behind her.

"It shouldn't be too hard to track," she said.

"Because of the blood from its foot wound?"

Maga grimaced as her hands met a mucous covered tree trunk. She shook the slime from her fingers and looked back to Manchester with a frown. "Not exactly."

CHAPTER 14
MIGHTY TEMBO

The thundering sneezes echoed through the forest, less frequent now, but still unnerving in their volume and ferocity. Maga turned about to make certain the others yet followed her. The four humans and lone Áes dána fumbled through the dark, stumbling over roots and running afoul briars and thickets.

"Perhaps a will-o'-wisp or torch?" she offered, as she took Manchester's hand to guide him.

"No," he said. "I don't want the creature to notice us."

"What the elephant doesn't hear, the lion will smell," Maga said.

"Or the monkey will see," Manchester said. "Or the snake will taste." The king groaned, rubbing his back and cringing. "There is an entire circus out there, after all."

Maga gently rubbed her husband's back, her silver eyes gazing ahead through the ravaged forest. "That was a big fall you took," she said with worry. "Are you certain you're up to this?"

"No one would think you less a man if you went back to camp," Pope added.

"Is no shame," Pfeil said. "You fought well. Rest now."

"I'm fine," Manchester said with a wave of his hand. "Just...."

A dark, simian shape dropped from the trees, landing on Manchester's back, knocking off his hat, and rolling with him onto the forest floor. "What did you do to mighty Tembo?" it shrieked as it balled its hand into a fist and struck Manchester on the jaw. The creature was roughly half Manchester's size, yet its strength was fierce and unrelenting. It battered him with the other fist, its mouth dripping with rabid foam and its eyes wide with madness.

Not wanting to risk hitting her husband with sword or arrow, Maga grasped the creature by the shoulders, struggling to pull it away. It screeched and howled, resisting Maga's pull by digging its grasping ape-feet into Manchester's wrists. Pope and Pfeil lent their strength to the struggle, and finally, with all of their might, they wrested the fiend from Manchester.

Maga could finally get a good look at the creature, seeing that it possessed elements of chimpanzee and some breed of canine. It hissed, spat, and growled as Maga, Pope, and Pfeil attempted to restrain it. "I will die for mighty Tembo!" it cursed. "I will kill for mighty Tembo!" Pope's men joined the fray, circling the creature with a length of rope. It struggled and bit and snapped, but between the five of them, they bound it securely.

Sweating from her exertions, Maga crouched down beside the squirming creature, placing her sword blade at its throat. "I urge you to stop struggling," she panted. "This blade is quite sharp. I would hate for you to cut yourself on it."

The beast went still, glaring at Maga with bloodshot eyes. "Kill me," it spat. "I have failed mighty Tembo. I deserve to die."

"Who is mighty Tembo?" Manchester groaned as he staggered to his feet.

The trees behind them splintered, and the hunting party turned about in alarm. The soft glow of a will-o'-wisp illuminated the forest, revealing the giant elephant-lion, as well as a bear-gorilla, and a tiger-python. And at the lead, holding the will-o'-wisp in one hand and a blood tipped arrow in the other, stood a rather sheepish, yet familiar black and white dog-cat-boy.

"Riley?" Maga said. She darted from the captive chimp creature and moved towards the other circus patchworks. "Get away from them!" she ordered Riley.

Pope and his men drew their guns, and Pfeil readied his bow. Manchester placed his hands on his pistol hilts, but stood his ground.

"There is no need for further violence," the elephant-lion said in a deep, rumbling bass that held everyone captive. "Your ward has explained how his arrow hit me by accident. He has removed the arrow from between my toes. The wound is not serious and will heal."

"So, young Androcles removed the thorn from the lion's paw," Manchester chuckled, slumping into a relaxed posture.

"You shouldn't have left camp, Riley," Maga scowled, ignoring her husband's mirth.

"Maybe if you had listened to us, we could have told you why Tembo was so enraged," Riley replied. "It was our arrow. It was our responsibility."

"That is good bogenschiessen," Pfeil nodded.

"Oh, shut up," Maga said, glaring in Pfeil's direction. "He doesn't need any more encouragement."

"Like you've ever given us any," Riley grumbled, wiping Tembo's blood from his arrow and placing it back in his quiver.

Maga felt a churning sickness in her stomach. Her eyes went soft as she looked to Riley. Riley glared back at her, his eyes every bit as piercing as his arrows. She sheathed her sword and turned away.

Manchester stepped forward, clearing his throat in an awkward attempt to change the subject. "Mighty Tembo, is it?" he said with a bow. "I am King Martin of Willow Prairie."

"I am aware of who you are, King Martin," Tembo said, lowering his tremendous girth in reply. "We were on our way to Willow Prairie when our train derailed."

Manchester moved closer, his face creased with curiosity and concern. "Did you see who was responsible? Was it a pale woman?"

"Yes," Tembo said, cocking his massive head with surprise. "A witch. She was attended by animal men who kidnapped the passengers and circus animals." Tembo bent his head, as if it was weighed down by some nightmare memory. "She did this to us."

"But mighty Tembo fought for our freedom!" the chimpanzee creature blurted.

Tembo chuckled, a deep and throaty mirth. "Loyal Fitz," he said. "Yes, I saved those I could, but the witch fled before we could make her pay for her crimes."

"Can you tell us where you last saw her?" Maga asked.

"It is a cursed place," Tembo replied with a halting voice. "An old manor house built upon Nagonene bones."

"Is it far from here?"

Tembo shook his head. "Only a mile or so through the forest. I can lead you there. But be warned, it is a place drenched in nightmares."

"If Ollamh Cron has returned," Manchester said, "we have more to worry about than Nagonene ghosts. Lead on."

"Of course," Tembo said. He raised his trunk and motioned to his bound comrade. "But please release my friend, Fitz."

Maga nodded. She walked over to the wallowing creature, bent down, and cut the rope with her knife. The chimp-dog bolted up, hissed at Maga, and scurried over to hide behind Tembo's leg.

"Follow us," Tembo said, motioning with his trunk as he and his patchworks lumbered into the forest.

Riley lingered, looking to Maga, a sudden sadness in his eyes.

Maga smiled to him. "I'm sorry," she whispered, just loud enough for him to hear.

Riley smiled back, his tongue lolling out the side of his mouth and his tail wagging as he trotted over to her. She bent down to run her hands through his fur and kiss the top of his head. "I may not say it enough, but I'm very proud of you, my little prince," she said.

Manchester walked up to them, dusting off his top hat and placing it securely on his head. "Do you think I should get some kind of strap for this?" he asked.

CHAPTER 15
WHERE EVIL SLEEPS

As the king's party followed the circus patchworks through the thick Ohio wilderness, Riley watched Fitz closely. The cat in Riley found Fitz's lack of grooming repulsive... one could embrace one's animal nature and still avoid mange, fleas, and other parasites. And then there was the way Fitz walked... his knuckles dragging on the ground as if his arms were all meat and no bones. Exceedingly bad form... no self-respecting archer would ever treat his hands in such a careless fashion. Finally, the stench. Riley's sensitive nose caught all manner of foul aromas wafting from Fitz's mangy hide... feces, dead animal carcasses, whiskey. Truly this was an unworthy creature. Tembo had called him "Loyal Fitz," but Riley suspected the wretch clung to the giant patchwork less out of loyalty and more out of self-preservation.

The forest thinned and surrendered to a vast stretch of rolling hills. At the top of the highest mound stood a skeletal house, eerie and empty against the diffused moonlight. It seemed to wink at them as shadows and light danced through its windows. Riley felt a tingle of fierce caution trickle down his spine, raising his hackles and setting his mouth into a snarl.

Maga noticed his unease and set her hand upon his head. "Do you wish to stay here while we go ahead?"

Riley glanced over at Fitz who hovered near Tembo. The chimp sneered at the ratcatcher, seeming to sense his discomfort.

"No," Riley said to Maga. "We shall go with you."

Maga nodded and smiled, moving ahead to talk to Manchester.

Riley stayed back a moment, removing an arrow from his quiver and nocking it to his bowstring.

"You nervous," Pfeil noted as he walked next to Riley. "Archer does not ready arrow unless he expect to use."

"There is witchcraft at work here," Riley hissed as he nodded towards the dark manor house.

"Witch leave in hurry," Pfeil shrugged. "Make sense she leave some craft behind."

"And we are all in danger because of it," Riley replied.

As they approached the house on the hill they saw the evidence of Tembo's great rescue mission littering the area. The nearby barn had been flattened, just a few timber beams and the stonework foundation jutting through the scattered wreckage. A barred window, still attached to a large 10 foot section of brick wall, was discarded near a matching hole in the wall of the house. And through the hole the dim moonlight revealed the shadowed remains of Cron's laboratory.

Manchester and Maga cautiously stepped inside, their feet grinding into the broken glass and shards of masonry. Pope and his men stood outside, standing guard with their guns at the ready. Tembo and his patchworks hovered a few yards away from the house, stamping their feet nervously, save for Fitz who merely hunched near Tembo and glared into the dark house. Riley padded in behind Maga and Manchester, mindful of the glass, his bow lowered but ready at a moment's notice. Pfeil followed Riley inside, holding the will-o'-wisp, its warm light bathing the laboratory in orange and yellow.

The smell of chemicals stung Riley's nose, almost overpowering him. The light danced over large tubes and tanks filled with translucent green liquid, their glass bulks bolted to the walls with iron straps. Inside dead things floated... abandoned experiments... half finished patchworks, some part man, others part Áes dána, and even part dwarf and part goblin.

"She's experimenting with new subjects," Maga noticed as she gazed into the tubes.

Riley's foot hit a small metal object, sending it skittering a few feet until it stopped near a pile of discarded clothing. Riley crept to the pile, poking it with the tip of his arrow, moving the cloak away to see what lie beneath. His eyes widened. "Queen," he called in an urgent whisper.

Maga looked to him. "What is it?"

Riley pointed to the pile, showing her the armor beneath the cloak.

Maga gasped. "Dragon bride armor." Her pace fueled by panic, Maga rushed to the opening in the wall. She looked to Tembo with pleading eyes. "There was a dragon bride here?" she asked.

Tembo shook his huge, maned head. "I don't know," he said. "It was chaos the night we drove the witch away. Some of the patchworks followed her. Others scattered into the darkness. Only Fitz, Yuri, and Anna joined me."

Manchester called back to Maga. "There's something here you should see."

Maga lowered her eyes with worry and turned about. She walked up to Manchester who hovered over a desk strewn with papers. Pfeil stood over his shoulder, holding the will-o'-wisp.

"Her notes," Manchester said, motioning to the papers.

"Cannot read," Pfeil added as he turned to Maga. "But recognize language. Is your people."

Maga's eyes widened as she looked over the documents. "It's Dragon!"

"Why would Cron be writing in Dragon?" Manchester mused.

Maga took up one of the pages, scanning it frantically. "She's written the same thing, over and over." Her mouth and tongue seemed to meditate a moment, as if preparing for some task they had not performed for a long, long time. *"Durm taln nawneev larnawl kir har anduv durm,"* she intoned.

Riley glanced through the gap in the wall. Fitz's face spread into a wide grin, his yellow eyes growing round with madness. He danced at Tembo's feet. *"Durm taln nawneev larnawl kir har anduv durm,"* he said in imitation. *"Durm taln nawneev larnawl kir har anduv durm."*

Riley drew back his bow, aiming the arrow at Fitz's chest. "Mighty Tembo," he said, "we suggest you move away from Fitz."

Tembo looked down to the chimp-dog who continued to gibber near his feet. "But it's only Fitz."

"This is no longer Fitz," Riley said, keeping his arrow on target.

Maga, Manchester, and Pfeil turned away from the desk and looked to Riley and the evolving incident outside. Maga moved swiftly to Riley's side. "Riley," she started, her tone soothing and soft, "are you certain?"

"Durm taln nawneev larnawl kir har anduv durm," the creature repeated, his pitch growing fevered and shrill. Foam flecked from his mouth and his eyes rolled back in his head, showing only bloodshot white.

Riley looked to Maga with upraised brow. Maga nodded in reply.

With swift, unsettling movement, Fitz clambered up Tembo's back and sprang from the top of the giant's head, landing on the peek of the manor house. There he huddled near the weather vane, gibbering and laughing like some mad child with a silly joke looping through his head. *"Durm taln nawneev larnawl kir har anduv durm,"* he babbled.

Riley ran out the hole in the wall and stood on the lawn. He redirected his arrow to the roof. As he prepared to let loose his arrow, the ground heaved beneath him. His aim fouled, Riley's arrow flew off into the night, missing Fitz and lodging into the roof beside him. The ground continued to undulate and break as skeletal hands erupted from the soil, sending the travelers scattering. Pope and his men jumped and yelled like schoolboys who'd run afoul a rattlesnake. They fired their guns at the ground in random panic, nearly hitting each other in the boots, yet doing nothing to halt the slow, terrifying rebirth of the Nagonene dead.

Dozens of the skeletons now shambled free of the earth, advancing on their living quarry. With a loud trumpet of his trunk, Tembo waded into the column of undead, his great girth pulverizing and splintering their ranks. The bear-gorilla and tiger-python leapt into battle behind their leader, savage animal claws and gnashing predator jaws scraping bones and cracking skulls. Pope and his men, having found their bullets useless, now battered the fiends with the butts of their pistols and rifles. Maga stormed out of the house, waving her sword, severing the chattering skulls from their vertebrae. Manchester and Pfeil rushed from the house as well, Pfeil using his bow as a club while Manchester wrapped his hand in his leather belt did his best *"Gentleman Jim" Corbett* homage.

Riley ignored the undead attackers, scurrying to the trellis on the side of the house. He clambered up the side, his bow slung on his back. As he reached the roof he saw Fitz, still chanting the strange words, mouth now dry and cracked, eyes filling with blood, and body trembling. Riley now felt sorry for the creature. And in that pity he found the conviction to free the wretch from Cron's witchcraft. He drew his bow and released the arrow. The ratcatcher's aim was true, his arrow piercing Fitz's heart and sending the chimp-dog slumping over. His tongue now still, the creature stared at Riley, eyes growing dim as tears of blood stained gray cheeks. Riley lowered his eyes. He may have not cared for Fitz, but the creature was still one of his own... a patchwork.

Riley looked over the edge of the roof, hoping to see the undead army fall now that their cantor was dead. And yet, they still advanced. Even the ones already slain reformed and attacked anew. Riley reached for the tomahawk tied to his belt, intending to climb down to join the fray. A hot, rank breath stirred the fur on the back of his neck. The ratcatcher turned just in time to see Fitz's black and empty eyes and feel his grasping monkey paws on his throat. *"Durm taln nawneev larnawl kir har anduv durm,"* the fiend gurgled. Riley loosed the tomahawk and swung it around to batter the side of Fitz's head. The chimp's head wobbled and his lips split into a blood-caked grin. *"Durm taln nawneev larnawl kir har anduv durm."* With a growl and grunt, Riley rolled over with Fitz, sending both tumbling from the roof and hurdling to the living graveyard below. Fitz took the brunt of the impact... Riley could feel the chimp's bones snap and pop as he landed on top of him. Dark blood spurted from the creature's mouth and nose, yet he continued to chant. *"Durm taln nawneev larnawl kir har anduv durm."*

Soon the undead Nagonene joined him, their tongueless skulls echoing with the eerie mantra. *"Durm taln nawneev larnawl kir har anduv durm."*

One of Pope's men fell beneath over a dozen of the skeletons, their clanking, clacking mass too much for him. Pope kicked at the mass of bones, snapping femur and humerus, shattering skull and pelvis. By the time he and the other soldier pried the clattering horde from their comrade, he arose dead-eyed and expressionless. *"Durm taln nawneev larnawl kir har anduv durm,"* the soldier moaned. Pope and his man backed away, guarding themselves with their rifles as they stalked back towards the house.

Maga, Manchester, and the patchworks had been herded back towards the manor as well. Only mighty Tembo stayed on the lawn, scattering bones with his great trunk and smashing skulls with his thundering feet.

Pfeil pulled Riley from Fitz. "Leave the monkey," the big Áes dána said. "We gather at house."

"Let us finish him!" Riley protested.

"How can you kill what is already dead?" Pfeil asked, taking the young patchwork under one arm as he swung his bow at the advancing Nagonene with the other. With four long strides, he backed his way to the house, letting Riley down beside Maga.

"The Noggle Lord destroyed the Smith's undead at Tamarack," Maga said frantically to Manchester. "Can't you summon him again?"

"Not without Bugbear," Manchester said with a shake of his head. "And even then, I doubt we could recreate the exact circumstances to assemble him again."

"Then there's no hope," Maga grunted, swinging her sword at the advancing corpses.

Manchester's head cocked as though suddenly stuffed with something Bugbear would think. "*Hope*! That's it!" Manchester quickly kissed Maga's cheek. "Cover me," he blurted as he ducked back into Cron's laboratory.

Maga nodded as her sword cleaved an advancing skeleton clavicle to coccyx.

Riley padded after the king. "Can we help?"

"Fetch me the will-o'-wisp," Manchester said as he rifled through the papers on Cron's desk.

Riley scurried up to the king, the will-o'-wisp in hand. Manchester received it with a nod. He quickly removed his royal

quill from his inside vest pocket... Riley knew the king was never
without the relic that birthed his reign. Dipping it in Cron's inkwell,
Manchester scrawled a strange, yet familiar symbol on the paper.
Anxiously blowing it dry, he then wrapped it about the will-o'-wisp.
He held it towards the wall, where Riley could see the symbol cast in
shadow and light.

Manchester grimaced to Riley as he tucked the quill back into his
vest pocket. "Stand back, son. If this doesn't work, run back to camp
and tell Tudmire to lead everyone back to Willow Prairie."

Riley nodded and watched as the king ran towards the hole in the
wall. He held out the will-o'-wisp, the strange symbol now cast out at
the vast sea of writhing bones. As the light hit the undead, they
collapsed, melting back into the ground like sugar in the rain. Even
Pope's man fell, the color returning to him and the spark of life
flickering in his eyes. Manchester waded into the midst of the falling
undead army, the light like scissors cutting marionette strings.

Finally, only Fitz remained, snarling and spitting at Tembo's feet.
"Durm taln nawneev larnawl kir har anduv durm," the chimp
shrieked. Tembo raised his foot and brought it down on the creature,
pinning him to the ground as Manchester's symbol fell over the
chimp's startled face like a shadowy shroud. Slowly, Fitz relaxed, his
face easing into a soft and contented smile. "I would die for the
Baymaari," he rattled. "You shall die for them too." The creature's
eyes dulled into a milky dead stare as the life flowed from his body
in a cloud of gray dust that rose into the night and evaporated.

Maga cautiously prowled across the lawn, approaching
Manchester. She surveyed the now green and empty lawn. "What
did you do?" she asked him, amazement and admiration coloring
her voice.

Manchester pulled the paper from the will-o'-wisp and handed it to her. "When you mentioned hope, I remembered," Manchester said. "Same Non-Logical word the Noggle Lord wrote on the Shadow Smith's head."

Maga beamed at Manchester and leapt into a kiss... a very long and passionate kiss... the kind that at first brought smiles to the faces of those who watched, but soon caused all manner of uncomfortable coughs, and hem-haws, and shuffling feet, and downward glances. When Maga finally broke the kiss she gazed deeply into her husband's eyes. "You're brilliant."

"If that's what a man gets for being smart, we hope to stay stupid," Riley grumbled to himself.

A low moan drew eyes towards Tembo. The giant knelt down beside the still body of Fitz, his trunk gently running over the dead patchwork's mangy pelt. "I have dim memories of my human life," Tembo started, wet circles pooling beneath his eyes. "I was the train conductor. The railroad kept badgering me about keeping the hobos out of the boxcars. But I never listened. Fitz and his mangy dog were regulars on my route. I don't remember if we were close friends or not. But I do remember he was always grateful that I let him stay." Tembo stopped stroking the still body and stood. "If I'd listened to the railroad, Fitz would be alive today."

"Ollamh Cron is to blame for this, not you," Manchester said. "She unleashed the evil that possessed your friend."

"Then my pride and I shall hunt her down," Tembo said, wiping away the tears with his trunk. "We shall make her pay."

"Her original laboratory was in the old ruins of Eglwys Cacynen," Manchester offered. "I imagine she'll return there to regroup. We have maps of the area back at our camp. You're welcome to them."

Tembo nodded his great head. "We shall bury Fitz and join you shortly."

The night began to break, black fading to orange-gray as the sun danced on the edge of the world. The king's party trudged down the hill as behind them the patchworks dug a grave for their fallen comrade.

"You brave boy," Pfeil said to Riley as he walked up beside him and playfully tousled the fur on top of his head. "Dive into danger like duck into water."

Riley turned to the big Áes dána, wagging his tail. "Sometimes we think danger dives into us."

"But you still cant bow when you shoot," Pfeil lectured with upraised finger. "Keep bow straight when possible."

"But Maga taught us to cant the bow," Riley said.

"Maga teach you to shoot like warrior," Pfeil said. "Pfeil teach you to shoot like champion. Both good. She help you kill zombie monkeys. Pfeil help you win tournaments. Is deal?"

Riley held out his hand, and the Áes dána took it in a firm grasp. "Is deal," the patchwork smiled.

"We start lessons again when back to camp," Pfeil nodded.

Riley nodded in return and trotted ahead to Maga and Manchester. He could overhear them speaking of serious things, so rather than interrupt and tell them of his new archery tutor, he walked silently beside them.

"What did those words mean?" Manchester asked Maga as they trod the forest trail. "The ones in Dragon that Cron had written?"

Maga swallowed, her silver eyes growing slightly dim. *"You cannot fight what is inside you."*

"Could this have something to do with this mysterious threat Bugbear is searching for?" Manchester wondered aloud.

"It's a good bet," Maga said. "Raising the dead, mind control, hopelessness. All tactics the Shadow Smith used. Makes sense his masters would employ the same methods. And it would explain how Cron has returned after being killed at Tamarack."

Manchester sighed. "I hope Bugbear's travels lead him along safer trails than ours."

Maga laughed. "I'm sure he's sipping lemonade in a library somewhere, unraveling the mysteries of the universe and stitching them back together to suit his fancy."

Manchester chuckled. "And no doubt as he does, he's driving everyone around him crazy."

CHAPTER 16
A TIME TO HEAL... A TIME TO LEARN

Asherby tugged at his dark hair as he leaned on the stone bench. "You drive me crazy," he said to Bugbear.

The goblin waddled over the flat stepping stones as the morning sun streamed between the tall stone monoliths that circled the throne room. "If that's true it will be nice to have some company."

"That creature could have killed you last night," Asherby grumbled. "As you so consistently remind me, it's my fault that you're without your Non-Logical Thought. I feel somewhat responsible for your safety."

"Why, Asherby," Bugbear chuckled. "What would your masters in Washington think if they knew you'd grown so attached to a goblin?"

"I'm not 'attached' to you," Asherby smirked as he hobbled to his feet, leaning on his banderberry cane. "But I'd just as soon not have to dig your grave."

"Well, of course. Wouldn't want to ruin that manicure of yours."

Asherby opened his mouth to offer a retort, but the sudden shuffle of boots on stone drew their attention to the garden entrance. Threelgon and several guards ushered Brenen through the archway, shoving him to the ground.

"Ah yes," Bugbear snorted. "Have a productive meeting with Rígan?"

Brenen remained on the ground, his eyes narrow and still. "I am to be seneschal."

"Well," Bugbear said with a grin. "That's a plum position. My cousin is a seneschal, you know."

"I am to be seneschal to her mews," Brenen added in a creaking, emotionless voice.

"Does that mean he feeds her birds?" Asherby asked Bugbear.

"Yes," Bugbear snickered. "And cleans up after them too."

"I imagine a queen like her has a big collection of birds," Asherby added.

"Oh yes," Bugbear nodded. "A big collection with lots of droppings."

Brenen sat up and sighed. "If you two are finished celebrating my downfall, her majesty has requested your presence in the healing gardens."

"Excellent!" Bugbear piped. "You can have that game leg of yours looked at, Asherby."

Threelgon motioned the pair through the archway and guided them down the forest trail.

In a glen where a small stream cascaded down a small wall of rocks into a small pool of clear, still water, Rígan waited. She dipped her bare toe into the pool as she twined the fingers on her single hand through her red curls. The queen raised her azure eyes to meet Threelgon, Bugbear, and Asherby as they approached.

"Your majesty," Bugbear said with a deep bow.

Asherby followed in awkward imitation. "Uhm, likewise."

Rígan laughed. "You are not used to royalty, are you, Mister Asherby?"

"No, ma'am," Asherby answered. "A few diplomatic functions back in D.C. But I'm mostly a military man."

"Well, dear sir," Rígan said as she patted the large rock beside her, urging him to sit, "if you were familiar with royalty, you'd find yourself unfamiliar with me."

"Don't follow, ma'am," Asherby said as he hobbled over and gently eased himself down onto the rock.

Rígan smiled as she tenderly rolled up the tall man's pant leg. "I'm not your typical queen. I don't stand on formality, and don't have much time for those who do. We live a hard life out here away from the cushy Áes dána courts. If we were to indulge in all of the pretenses and rituals they did, we would starve." Rígan examined the leg, running her fingers along Bugbear's makeshift suture. "This is good work, goblin."

"I did the best I could," Bugbear said, sniffing a large flower, "considering someone had robbed me of my connection to Non-Logical Thought."

Asherby grumbled.

"We have learned much of healing in our exile," Rígan said. "Unfortunately, the unseelie curse does not allow us to heal ourselves. But we do what we can to help others." Rígan took Asherby's hand. "Dip your hands into the pool, Mister Asherby."

Asherby shrugged and cupped his hands into the clear pool. As he brought up the handful of water, Rígan gently blew into it. She then lay her hand over Asherby's hands and urged him to lower them towards the wound.

"Release the water over the wound," she instructed.

Asherby did so. He winced as smoke rose from the puncture. And yet as the smoke cleared and the water dripped away, the wound miraculously faded and the thread from the sutures fell to the ground.

"How did you do that?" he asked, his face painted with confusion.

"I did not," Rígan replied. "We did."

Asherby smirked, and Rígan returned the smile.

"One wound down," Bugbear said. "An entire world to go."

"Oh," Rígan started as though suddenly remembering Bugbear's presence, "I had a chance to look at Brenen's wound as well."

Bugbear froze, his face skewered into something between shame and shock. "You, you did?"

"Yes," the queen said, standing and walking over to the goblin. "Very serious. Not much I could do for him except change the dirty bandages."

"Well," Bugbear fidgeted, "yes, I imagine so. What with the cannons and gunfire and all that. Lucky to have escaped with his life."

"What is your game, goblin," Rígan bent down and whispered for only Bugbear to hear.

"I'm not sure yet," Bugbear whispered in return. "But I have a feeling you and Brenen are two of the most important pieces."

Rígan rose and regarded Bugbear with narrow eyes and a canny smile. "Tread carefully, scholar."

"Speaking of scholars," Bugbear chirped, attempting to change the subject, "may I see that library now?"

Rígan smirked and removed a tattered scroll from her belt. "I've done your research for you," she said, handing the parchment to Bugbear. "This is the most ancient Coranieid chronicle in existence. I believe there is a line in there relevant to our conversation with your gardener."

Bugbear quickly snatched the scroll, his hungry eyes devouring every word in a matter of seconds. "But this is... it's madness!"

Asherby stood, stomping the foot of his formerly wounded leg and exhaling with relief. "Good as new," he said. He strode over to peer over Bugbear's shoulder. "What's madness?"

Bugbear looked up to Asherby with irritation. "It's a Coranieid record," he sputtered. "Ancient, rare, and beyond your comprehension!"

"Sorry," Asherby huffed.

"It says: *After much struggle and toil the masters have finally claimed the life of a dragon,*" Rígan recited as she placed a hand on

Asherby's shoulder.

"That is not a precise translation," Bugbear corrected. "They didn't *claim* a dragon's life. They *usurped* it."

"What's the difference?" Asherby asked.

Bugbear poked a finger into Asherby's St. George medal. "They became the dragon!" Bugbear waddled back and forth beside the pool, his mind racing and bubbling. He removed the red leather tome from his coat pocket and flipped through the pages. He stopped as he came to the page with all of the notations and stars. "Here!" he blurted, showing the page to Asherby. *"During the cataclysm, the draugen were cast into the other world,"* Bugbear read aloud. He then stabbed each of the handwritten notes with his fingertip. *"Saint George. Plagues. The enemy within."*

"I don't understand," Asherby shrugged.

"I told you it was beyond your comprehension!" Bugbear exclaimed, slamming the book shut. "But I shall try to walk you through it. You don't have a game leg now, so there's no excuse for not keeping up." Bugbear began waddling down the garden path, Rígan and Asherby following. "Your human legends often depict dragons as evil, correct?"

Asherby nodded.

"Then let us assume these *draugen* were dragons that had somehow been *usurped* by the ancient enemy. While true dragons remained on Annwfn, the draugen were stranded on your world. Now looking at the most famous dragon legend of your world, St. George, we have that rather interesting tidbit about the dragon being *plague-bearing*." Bugbear turned to Rígan with upraised finger. "And what was the word Duergar used last night?"

"Baymaari," Rígan answered.

"Which means *plague*!" Bugbear expounded. "So, human history tells us that mankind began suffering a series of plagues shortly after George slew the dragon. What if this *Baymaari* was unleashed? What if it was responsible for the infamous Black Death that decimated Europe... a plague that seemed to bring with it an abundance of legends about vampires, werewolves, witches, and demons."

"That actually makes a lot of sense," Asherby said, "with what we've seen of these dead coming back to life and such."

Bugbear stomped Asherby's foot, sending the tall man hopping in pain.

"Ow!" he exclaimed. "Why did you do that?"

"This is my theory," Bugbear hissed as he poked a finger into Asherby's chest. "Do not contribute to it!"

Asherby held up his hands and snorted. "Fine." He turned to Rígan. "Might need you to take a look at that foot later."

Bugbear ignored Asherby and continued his lecture. "Only with the Renaissance was the plague halted. And even as other plagues cropped up here and there, always some great advance in learning, invention, or discovery seemed to stop them." Bugbear spun about raising his hands in triumph as he laughed to Rígan and Asherby. "Hope," Bugbear smiled. "Hope is what stopped the Baymaari. For you see, what we are facing is not a race of warriors, monsters, or wizards... but a culture of infection and disease. A sentient micro-empire that infects the weak, possesses the hopeless, animates the dead, and destroys what it cannot own. And the only cure, the only inoculation... is hope." Bugbear rocked back on his heels, his hands on his lapels, and a victorious grin on his lips. "Feel free to applaud."

Rígan wriggled her fingers. "One hand."

"Oh," Bugbear said, his arrogance suddenly deflated by shame. "Sorry."

Asherby lightly clapped his hands and smiled.

"Really!" Bugbear blurted, his tongue thick with offense. "The moment has passed, Asherby. Now you're just making a fool of yourself in front of the Queen!" The goblin stormed off, a stream of mumbled outrage trailing behind him.

Asherby stammered. "I... I just thought..."

Rígan smiled and patted the tall man on the cheek. "You're too cute," she giggled as she glided past him and down the trail where Threelgon waited.

A crooked grin crept up the right corner of Asherby's mouth as he stumbled after her. "She said I was cute," he nodded to Threelgon.

The tall unseelie warrior glowered. Asherby tapped him on the chest. "I'm sure she thinks you're cute too."

Threelgon silently fell in behind Asherby, Rígan, and Bugbear as they exited the healing gardens.

CHAPTER 17
FUGITIVES

Brenen wheezed and coughed as he stopped to look over his shoulder. The forest stretched behind him, nothing but trees and bramble in his sight. No one had followed him. No one had seen him escape. His scheme to distract his guards with pebbles and thrown voices worked better than he had expected. He wiped the sweat from his brow and slumped against a tree, grateful that unseelie wits had been dulled by years of isolation.

And yet Brenen was unseelie now as well, his escape little more than a brief holiday before being dragged back to a torturous fate. He could never return to an Áes dána court, not even as a servant. Knowing of the unseelie code, no other races would offer him sanctuary either. Unless... the humans. Asherby had said his people would give him a medal for being wounded in battle. Brenen's wound was from battle as well. Perhaps, just perhaps, in their glorification of such indignities they would find some worth in him. Living among roughhewn humans for the remainder of his days hardly seemed ideal, but it was certainly preferable to cleaning up owl droppings.

He closed his eyes and relaxed for a few moments, his fingertips dancing across the moss-covered tree roots and his lungs taking in the clean, forest air. He could understand the unseelie attraction to such wild surroundings. A flock of birds scattered from the nearby treetops, their shrill calls echoing through the forest. A ground squirrel darted for a hole at the base of a cluster of ferns. And the earth itself seemed to hum with life. Actually, it seemed more like a rumble. No, definitely a tremble.

Brenen opened his eyes as the tremors grew more violent. Down the way the trees shook and great throaty yells roared like thunder.

A cloud of dust and debris rolled towards him. Brenen had heard tales of such things, rare as they were. It was an ogre stampede, and it was not something one wanted to experience up close.

Brenen ran from the approaching cloud, his weak and knobby legs pumping like pistons on a steam train. His lungs were still burning from his initial escape effort, but he forced himself to keep running. Unfortunately, it seemed the stampede was guiding him right back in the direction of the unseelie court. But just as a mundane life with the humans was preferable to cleaning up owl droppings, cleaning up owl droppings was preferable to being ground to paste beneath ogre heels.

The cloud drew closer now, Brenen's frantic pace not frantic enough to evade the panicked ogres. He could hear their cries and curses as they approached.

"Loomis! Why for attackering us? We done nothering!"

"Excepetering Dubbin! He being the one whom breakering your favoritest gruel bowl!"

"Liaring! I does no such thing!"

"Durm taln nawneev larnawl kir har anduv durm."

Brenen gasped. "Oh no! It's got an ogre!" He tried to force his legs to run faster, but they had reached their limit. He could feel the debris from the ogre stampede flicking and sprinkling the back of his neck and shoulders.

"Look out, Dubbin!" one of the ogres cautioned. "It be one er them little ass dandies!"

Brenen cringed. He hated the way the ogre tongue mutated his civilization's noble name.

"Out er our ways, little ass dandy!" the other one ordered. "Our brudder has a teriblous tempering!"

"Durm taln nawneev larnawl kir har anduv durm," the pursuing

ogre chanted.

The two ogres began passing Brenen on either side, their dust starting to obscure Brenen's vision and invading his throat. He coughed and sputtered, impeding his progress even more.

"Look!" Dubbin exclaimed. "More little ass dandies!"

"And our little gobling friend!"

Brenen slowed down even more as through the dust and debris he saw Bugbear, Asherby, Rígan, and a cluster of unseelie warriors standing in the path of the rampage. "What are you doing?" he called to them between coughs. "It's a stampede! Run!"

But they did not run. Instead Bugbear turned his back to Brenen and stood before the group, raising his hands like a symphony conductor. "One," the goblin said, the ogres growing ever closer. "Two," he said, the ogres nearly upon them. "Three!" he shouted as the two ogres ran to either side of them. The group jumped up in unison, their feet hitting the ground at the exact same time.

Brenen felt the breath of the mad ogre on the back of his neck.

"Durm taln nawneev larnawl kir har anduv durm."

And yet as the feet of the unseelie warriors met the ground, the vibrations seemed to hum through the earth, splintering forth, and piercing some brittle substrata beneath. The earth cracked and disintegrated beneath the ogre and Brenen. Both lost their footing, the ogre tumbling down into a deep chasm, while Brenen caught the edge of the fissure and clung for dear life.

As the dust settled, Bugbear waddled up to Brenen, his face full of self-congratulation. "As you can see my connection to Non-Logical Thought has returned," he explained. "I was able to orchestrate the vibrations from our feet to knock lose the decaying masonry and support beams from an old Underground Railroad tunnel."

"And the rampaging ogres had nothing to do with it?" Brenen

said.

"Well," Bugbear sniffed, "they might have helped. But it took just the right vibration at just the right pitch and frequency to really get the job done. Fortunately, I'm quite the expert in such harmonic sciences."

"Wonderful," Brenen sputtered and gasped as he struggled to pull himself up. "How about helping me out?"

"No," Bugbear said, shaking his head. "No, no." And with that, the goblin toddled away.

Rígan approached Brenen and held out her hand. "Your escape plan seems to have some holes," she smirked.

Brenen hesitantly accepted her hand and clambered out of the pit, kneeling on the ground and panting like a hound on an August hunt. "It wasn't a plan as much as an impulse."

"I suggest you resist such impulses in the future," she said firmly, her eyes violet slits. "Or the next time, we won't come after you." Rígan turned away from the disgraced king, walking to Bugbear and Asherby as they questioned the ogre brothers.

Brenen slumped with a contradictory mix of relief and dread. He peered down into the pit and shivered as he heard the echoes stirring below.

"Durm taln nawneev larnawl kir har anduv durm."

CHAPTER 18
SAVING LOOMIS

As they struggled to tell their tale Dubbin and Nigel sobbed, their bodies great quivering mounds of grief. Bugbear, Asherby, and Rígan gathered about them, faces set with compassion and calm.

"The king-boss done tellered us to be killering the Barghest while he and the queen-boss travelered to Warshington Deep Sea," Dubbin said.

"Washington?" Asherby said with surprise. "Why would your king want to go there?"

"Ass dancies and army sojourns come to Willow Prairie," Nigel said. "King-boss wantering to meeting wid Preserdent er Unitered Stateses to stoppering all er the fightering."

"Good man, Manchester!" Bugbear laughed. "Exactly what I would have advised him to do!" Then remembering the ogres' grief, the goblin settled into a more serious and supportive tone. "Now, tell us what happened to Loomis. Why was he chasing after you like that?"

"We doesn't knowing," Dubbin said. "We be goesing into woodses to huntering the Barghest. Afters two dayses we findering him slaughtsering other patchworks." Dubbin closed his eyes, tears squeezing through his eyelids and rolling down his purple cheeks.

"Loomis tellering him to stopsing," Nigel continued. "Barghest, he attacker us. Dubbin and me, we cans't be gettering in the mix. Loomis, he fightering too hardest and too fastest, beatering the Barghest with his fistses like hammerses."

"But as Barghest layering bleedsing on grounds," Dubbin said, "somethings happenering to Loomis. He beginnering to cries and he beginnering to shakes and he beginnering to falls to his kneeses."

"Loomis tellering him to stopsing. Barghest, he attacker us."

"The Barghest crawlsing away while we tends to Loomis," Nigel added. "When Loomis gettering up, he startsing to acts all addlepatted and speaksing gibberlish. We startses runnering and he startses chasering us."

Bugbear stroked his chin and turned to Asherby and Rígan. "For all of their bluster and rage, ogres actually aren't a violent people," the goblin mused. "I suspect, being recruited as a killer weakened Loomis' sense of self. It gave him a feeling of hopelessness."

"Which, if your theory is correct," Asherby said, "means Loomis was infected by the Baymaari."

"It is not a theory, Asherby!" Bugbear blurted. "It is a fact! And I suggest you accept that, lest you become the next one we're throwing in a pit!"

"Why are you suddenly being so antagonistic towards me?" Asherby asked as he held up his hands.

"Because," Bugbear growled with an upraised finger, "it is now apparent to me that we are racing headlong into dangerous events, even as those events are racing towards us! And it is imperative that you don't lag behind, Asherby. I'd rather be antagonizing you now than eulogizing you later."

Asherby frowned. "Okay then," he muttered, "the Baymaari are a fact." He pointed off to the gaping chasm in the middle of the forest. "And so is the rather large Baymaari infected ogre in that pit. What do you intend to do about him?"

Bugbear closed his eyes and sighed, one stark solution stabbing his mind like a knife of white heat. "I'll have a few words with him," the goblin said. He turned about to the gaggle of unseelie warriors. "Any of you lot bring a rope?"

Rígan gasped. "You intend to go in there with the brute?"

"That brute is a friend of mine," Bugbear grumbled, his voice buttered with indignant pride. "As are his brothers. I owe it to them to try to bring him back to sanity." Bugbear waddled towards the pit, peering down with wide and worried eyes. "I wouldn't let one of you rot down there either."

Threelgon approached, a length of rope in his hands. Bugbear nodded to the one-eyed warrior as he took one end of the rope and wrapped it about his waist.

"Can't you just use Non-Logical Thought to snap him out of it?" Asherby asked, a near frantic quaking in his voice as he drew towards Bugbear.

"The moving of events and altering of reality is a physical phenomenon, dear Asherby," Bugbear said as he secured the rope in a tight knot. "If I am to save Loomis, I must reach him on a purely

spiritual level. That requires a cunning mind and a faithful heart."
The goblin turned to Threelgon. "Hold steady, my friend. I shall try
to make this brief." And with a quick nod he lowered himself into the
pit.

As Bugbear reached the bottom, he unfastened the length of rope.
Dust-drenched streams of sunlight showered down from above,
revealing rubble and debris strewn across much of the immediate
area. Bugbear awkwardly struggled over splintered timbers and
slabs of shattered masonry, inching his way into the dark tunnel. He
could hear the rumble of Loomis' tortured breath, a lunatic's lullaby
to the darkness.

"Durm taln nawneev larnawl kir har anduv durm," the ogre
moaned.

Bugbear could not get a sense for Loomis' exact location, but he
at least knew he was within earshot. "Loomis, your brothers need
you," the goblin called out. And again in Dragon: *"Loomis, durmap
bruhai sullrath durm."*

"Durm taln nawneev larnawl kir har anduv durm," came the
reply.

"They are proud that you are not a killer," Bugbear announced.
"Whul hiryn fhir durm hiryn nawneev qirtul."

"Durm taln nawneev larnawl kir har anduv durm." The breath
and voice was closer now, perhaps only a matter of feet away.

"Your father is proud too," Bugbear said, spinning about like a
compass needle finding bearing in a sea of magnets. *"Durmap
wallurd har fhir bahir."*

"Durm taln nawneev..." The eerie mantra trailed off, a soft
sobbing creeping into its place. "Mine father?"

"Yes," Bugbear said quickly, seizing on the Baymaari's weakening
hold. "Yes. I visited the Ogre-Father recently. He told me that he

wishes to change the way the world sees ogres. Did you know that?"

A soft whimper came from the darkness. "Yes."

"Well, you have made a vital step towards that goal, Loomis," Bugbear continued. "In sparing the Barghest, you have shown traits of compassion, mercy, and civility beyond that of any other culture."

"But I be failering," Loomis sobbed. "I coulds nert killer the Barghest. I can *nawneev larnawl kir har anduv durm.*"

Bugbear panicked... the Baymaari were fighting back. "You are loved!" Bugbear shouted. *"Durm hiryn muhirt!"*

"Kuln muhirt...." The Dragon words stuck in his suddenly dry throat. Loomis swallowed and gasped, his breath heavy with emotion. "Whom lovers me?"

"Your brothers," Bugbear answered. "Your friends. Everyone who has ever had the pleasure of meeting you."

There followed a series of violent grunts and groans, as if Loomis wrestled with some great beast even larger than himself. He moaned and sobbed and with a final wretched gasp, he sighed. A thousand tiny screams seemed to float up into the air, and Bugbear could see small gray shapes mixing with the dust motes in the sunlight. They shimmered and swirled, until finally collapsing like tiny mud bubbles.

Loomis' big head moved into one of the wayward streams of light. His face was dripping with misery, yet also relief, as though a severe fever had suddenly broken. "Alwerays with such biggly lyings from sucha litter fella," he said with a weak laugh.

"Exaggerations, perhaps," Bugbear admitted with a smile. "But not lies."

Loomis huddled up beside Bugbear, pulling his knees under his chin and staring into the darkness. "What happenered to me, Bugbear?"

"You were infected," Bugbear said, sitting down beside the ogre. "You became susceptible during a moment of weakness and doubt."

"I hads er sicksness?"

"Yes," Bugbear said, patting the ogre's knee. "And I won't lie. It might come back. So, it's important that you remain strong. That you keep hope in your heart."

"That be soundering likes one er them thingies you be hatering so's muchly," Loomis smiled. "Whats er called... *clishee*?"

"A cliché?" Bugbear laughed. "Yes. I suppose it is a cliché. But it also happens to be the spiritual equivalent of chicken soup. So, eat hearty, Loomis. Eat hearty."

The ogre nodded as he starred down at his rumbling belly. "Remindering me. I hasn't eatsed fer a timely."

Bugbear chuckled as he reached into his inner coat pocket. He removed a leather wrap and sat it on a rock between them. He opened it and offered a large cookie to Loomis. "Snickerdoodle?"

"Snicker-does," Loomis replied as he accepted the cookie. The ogre took a bite and smiled. "I'm gladly to be seering you agin, Bugbear."

"I'm glad to see you again too, Loomis," Bugbear replied, taking a bite of snickerdoodle as one of the most genuine smiles he had ever known crossed his face.

Pfeil watched with amazement as Tembo moved the derailed locomotive back onto the railroad tracks. He used his massive head to push the great bulk, and then with his huge, oak-like arms and powerful trunk, he righted the engine and lowered it towards the tracks. Manchester and some of the soldiers guided the wheels onto the tracks using metal poles, but it was the mighty patchwork who did most of the labor.

"Easy," Manchester ordered. "To the left a bit. Don't fight the weight too much, boys. You'll snap the poles. Easy. Down. That's it."

The grooves on the train wheels gently eased onto the tracks, and the train was settled into place. Manchester congratulated his team of workers, and began consulting with the dwarf and his young human colleague.

Pfeil knew when he voyaged across the sea to visit Brenen's court that he would witness many rare and wonderful things. After all, in his native Alfheim the other races were practically non-existent. The goblins had migrated to Gaul to be near the sea and the warmer weather. The dwarves had long ago secluded themselves in their underground caverns and mines, digging ever deeper and ever further from daylight. And Pfeil's own ancestors had driven the ogres to the frozen wastes of Niflheim generations ago. Consequently, the archer had looked forward to seeing the diverse cultures of the West, and to share with them his passion for bogenschiessen.

Then, when the world suddenly became bigger and more vibrant during the Great Reunification, Pfeil's enthusiasm nearly exploded. Scouts and soldiers returned to court with fantastic tales of not only humans, but of strange creatures cobbled together from animals and men. Pfeil had urged Brenen to explore and reach out to these new neighbors, but the king dismissed the archer's interest in such diplomacy as pointless and unworthy. Pfeil could still feel the sting of the laughter in the banquet hall... twelve score of his western cousins jeering his "Old World" naiveté. He held his tongue after that, and before long became as jaded and cynical as his hosts.

But now, he had met humans. He traveled with them, ate with them, laughed with them. He had even matched wits with a notorious goblin trickster, and been lectured by a regal dragon bride. But most importantly, Pfeil had found someone who shared his passion for bogenschiessen... a patchwork youth whose blood seemed to sing with the nobility of the ancient Alfheim heroes. Here with the Ratcatcher he had found a closer kinship than even with his own cousins.

Pfeil watched with amusement as the youth darted in and out of one of the overturned boxcars, vexing his nursemaid, Tudmire.

"Get out here right now, young man!" the goblin ordered. "You have two more chapters to study!"

"Recess!" Riley shouted, sticking his tongue out at the fat goblin and darting back into the car.

Pfeil smiled as he stood beside Maga, who also watched. "Is good boy," he nodded to her.

"Well, he can be," she snickered. "But if his tormenting of poor Tudmire wasn't so funny, I'd be yelling at him myself."

"I sorry for putting nose where doesn't belong last night," Pfeil said. "You do good wid him. Teach him good bogenschiessen."

Maga smiled to the tall Áes dána. "Thank you. And I'm sorry if I was a little short with you earlier." Maga turned back to watch the playing patchwork. "When his godmother died last year, Martin, Bugbear, and I promised to look after him. I'm afraid I sometimes get a bit... *overly dramatic* when it comes to his well being."

"Is good you protect him," Pfeil said. "Boy is lucky to have family like yours."

Maga smiled and opened her mouth to reply... and then suddenly pressed her lips together as if holding in some dream she dare not reveal.

Manchester walked towards Maga, breathing from his exertions and mopping his forehead with a handkerchief. "Well, Bixby and Cobblestone say they can have the old 3:10 back up and running within the hour," he reported. "Tembo has set her heading east, and we've attached a passenger car for us and a cattle car for the horses."

"How long will it take us to get to Washington?" Maga asked.

"A little over a day."

"Amazing," Maga said shaking her head. "Would have taken another week on horseback."

Pfeil took in a deep breath and felt a thin shiver run through his frame as Tembo approached, his great footfalls booming like falling boulders. He towered over everyone and everything, and when he stood before them his shadow devoured their world. Pfeil did not fear the great patchwork, but he was certainly unnerved in his presence.

"Thank you again for the maps, your majesties," he said. "My pride and I shall do our best to hunt down the patchworker and put an end to her misery-making."

"And thank you for setting the train back on the tracks," Manchester said, offering his hand.

Tembo extended his trunk, gripping Manchester's hand and gently shaking it. "You will always have a friend in mighty Tembo. Call on me whenever you have need."

"And Willow Prairie shall always welcome you, mighty Tembo,"

Maga said with a bow. "The Great Drake be with you."

Tembo offered a shallow bow to Maga and Manchester. "And God be with you." The giant turned and raised his mighty trunk, blasting a thunderous roar into the morning air. His pride answered with their own lesser roars and fell in behind him as he followed the train tracks west.

"Well," Manchester said, turning to Maga, "let's get everything loaded while Bixby and Cobblestone fix the engine."

"Excellent," Maga replied. "It will be nice to get back on the move again."

"Are you sure is safe?" Pfeil asked, staring at the train through narrow eyes.

"Of course," Manchester said matter-of-factly. "People travel on trains all of the time."

"Went off track once," Pfeil shrugged. "Could happen again."

"We took extra care in making sure the wheels were securely on the tracks," Manchester explained, placing a reassuring hand on Pfeil's shoulder. "This train will travel as straight and true as one of your arrows."

"Then we certainly get to this Washington in less than day," Pfeil smirked.

It took several more ropes and a few log chains, but Dubbin and Nigel were able to pull Loomis from the pit. Dubbin hugged his brother, tears streaming down his face and emotion bubbling from his mouth. "Brudder!" he exclaimed. "So happily I is that you isn't tryering to killer me no more!"

"Shuts up with your gusherings," Loomis grumbled. "You be embarassering me in fronts of the unseemly ass dandies."

The unseelie warriors smiled as they gathered up the ropes and chains, apparently finding amusement in the ogres' butchering of their clan name. The ogre brothers joined them in cleaning up, while several other warriors posted signs warning of the pit.

"Now," Bugbear said to Rígan and Asherby, "since that tragedy has been averted, I'll bid you kind folk ado."

"Where are you going?" Asherby asked as Bugbear turned to walk away.

"To report my findings to my king," Bugbear answered. "I have a long walk to Washington, so if you'll excuse me."

"No need to walk, little man," Rígan laughed. "I'm more than happy to loan you a tylluan."

Bugbear spun about, amazement and disbelief claiming his face. "You have a tylluan?"

"No," Rígan corrected. "I have a parliament of tylluan."

Bugbear scampered up to her, his mouth curved with delight. "I haven't heard of such a thing since King Thesaron's time!"

"Would someone explain to me," Asherby started, "what a tyl... a tylliu... this thing is you're talking about?"

Bugbear took Asherby and Rígan by the hands and urged them forward. "It must be seen to be believed, dear Asherby," the goblin piped with excitement. "Come along, Rígan! Share this majestic treasure with us!"

Bugbear's enthusiasm fueling them, the trio soon made way back to the unseelie camp. Rígan led them to a circle of very large oak trees that seemed to stretch up, up, and up until their leaves tickled the bellies of the clouds. The queen looked to the sky, closing her eyes and inhaling deeply. Then she let out a soft, otherworldly trill, a sound that did not come from her body as much as from her soul. The treetops stirred, and Bugbear wrung his hands and fidgeted like a boy waiting for the candy shop to open. Shadows swirled overhead, dark shapes crossing over each other, slowly drawing closer and closer to the ground. Rígan opened her eyes and smiled, moving back towards the trees.

"I suggest you move back as well, gentlemen," she cautioned. "They sometimes have a difficult time with landings during the daylight."

Bugbear and Asherby eased back against the trees, watching with amazement as the dark shapes drew closer. Closer. Closer. And then, with a majestic rustle of feathers and a gentle chorus of soft *hoots*, twelve giant owls the size of bison landed on the forest floor.

"Great scott!" Asherby exclaimed. "No wonder Brenen ran away!"

"Please," Rígan whispered with a finger to her lips, "keep your voice down, Mister Asherby. They can be quite nervous around strangers."

Bugbear approached one of the tylluans, his eyes almost as big and round and theirs. He smiled small, not wanting to startle them by displaying his big, square teeth. They were owls after all, and the last thing Bugbear wanted was to trigger their predatory instincts with evidence of his rodent-like proclivity for grain and cheese. The giant raptor stirred slightly as Bugbear's fingers sifted through the thick feathers on its chest. Bugbear cooed softly, rubbing the great owl's chest and belly in a slow and soothing manner.

"These birds were the pride of the Áes dána Celestial Guard," Bugbear said softly to Asherby. "After the dragons left, the tylluans reigned supreme in the skies. No army could withstand an aerial assault by a squadron of these majestic war birds. Even the ogres trembled in their shadow." Bugbear turned from the owl and waddled over to Asherby. "They say King Thesaron's son got drunk one night and took one of the tylluans out for a ride. His saddle wasn't properly fastened and he fell to his death."

"Not to his death," Threelgon said, coming up from behind. "But close enough." The one-eyed warrior pulled a piece of dried venison from his pack, placing it in the beak of a grateful tylluan as he ruffled its feathered head. "After I was declared unseelie and banished from court, my father, maddened by grief, ordered all of the tylluans killed. Rígan was able to smuggle these few out of the kingdom without our father noticing. We unseelie have cared for them ever since... none more than me, so great is my guilt over my part in their near extinction."

"So, Rígan is your sister?" Asherby asked, as if that was the most important point of the story.

"Yes, human," Threelgon said with a wry grin. "I also have a brother named Gunther. Would you care to meet him? He's also rather *cute*."

Asherby chuckled nervously, looking to a beaming Rígan briefly before turning to Bugbear. "Have you ever ridden one of these before?" he asked the goblin.

"Heavens no," Bugbear replied. "As kind as Rígan's offer is, I fear I lack the skill to control such a magnificent animal. It seems I shall be walking after all."

"Nonsense," Threelgon said. "You'll ride with me."

"Are you certain?" Bugbear said with an upraised brow. "I mean, your accident...."

"I've made it a point to ride at least twice a week since," Threelgon answered. "And I haven't had a drink for over 200 years. I'm by far, the most accomplished and responsible tylluan rider in the colony."

Rígan came up behind Asherby and placed her hand on his shoulder. "And you can ride with me," she said. "I'm not quite as skilled as Threelgon, but I am better company."

Asherby turned to her, his eyes darting nervously. "I... I would be honored."

"Brenen must come as well," Bugbear said with smug certainty.

"Why is that?" Threelgon snorted.

"Why that is, is because I say that is," Bugbear grumbled.

"The goblin has a good point," Rígan interrupted. "It is part of Brenen's duties now, to look after the tylluans.."

"Excellent!" Bugbear said, rubbing his hands together. "They'll fly better during the evening, I'd wager. If we leave tonight, we should be in Washington by morning."

A clutch of unseelie guards broke through the oaks, Brenen in their custody. The former king gazed upon the parliament of tylluans with eyes half-closed in bitterness.

"Brenen!" Bugbear said. "Just in time. Feed and water the tylluans, and prepare three of them for flight. You'll be joining us."

Brenen sighed, his head hanging with heavy dread.

"Oh, don't look so down, Brenen," Bugbear said as he waddled up to the disgraced monarch. "There are a great many things that you'd find of interest in Washington, D.C. The Smithsonian Institution. The Library of Congress. Greed and corruption."

"Are you quite through mocking me?" Brenen hissed.

"Are you quite through being stupid?" Bugbear chuckled as he toddled past Brenen and through the tall oaks.

Threelgon thrust a shovel into Brenen's hands. "Don't forget to clean up the owl pellets," he growled.

"Pellets?" Brenen balked.

Asherby winced as he passed the owl-keeper. "Actually, they look more like small boulders to me."

CHAPTER 21
A MAN OF LETTERS

Bugbear's stomach churned. His mind cart wheeled. His heart thundered. Soon he would be traveling in the same manner as the kings of old. His shoulders would be draped in a mantle of clouds, his head crowned with a ring of stars, and his feet shod with the cool sensation of empty air. The earth would stretch beneath him, a mottled canvas of brown, green, and blue... a distant and trivial memory of a place he once meandered.

"You seem as nervous as me," Asherby said as he came upon Bugbear pacing in the healing gardens.

Bugbear turned about and smiled to the tall man. "Indeed. Finding out that the tylluans still exist is perhaps one of the most exciting discoveries I've ever made. It would be like a human explorer uncovering a lost herd of woolly mammoths."

"Not as elegant a mount as your tylluans, I'd imagine," Asherby snickered. The tall man let his mirth trickle to a sigh, his eyes grazing the ground in distraction.

Bugbear cocked his head, frowning as he read the human's face. "But I suspect you're nervous about something other than owls and elephants. Care to share?"

Asherby shuffled his feet, snorting and grinning in awkwardness as his gaze raced everywhere but towards Bugbear.

"Oh, Goodfellow's foot fungus," the goblin grunted. "I know that look. You're smitten!"

"No," Asherby chuckled as he waved dismissively at Bugbear. He laughed a bit longer before nervously clearing his throat and freezing his face into a wrinkled sheet of uncertainty. "Well, maybe."

"Rígan?" Bugbear nodded.

"She's..." Asherby started, waiting for his mind to catch up to his mouth... "amazing."

"Then tell her," Bugbear shrugged.

"I can't," Asherby replied. "She's a queen. I'm just a man."

Bugbear groaned, clearly uncomfortable with once again being tangled in affairs of the human heart, yet resigned to his unavoidable role as advisor. "I will tell you a story I have never shared with another soul, Asherby," the goblin began. "A story of my own true love." Bugbear closed his eyes and breathed deeply as he gathered his thoughts and courage. He opened his eyes and slowly looked to the sky.

"It was at the esteemed goblin university of Ysgol Gwybod that I met Zweenia, daughter of one if my instructors and the only other student who's genius approached my own."

"But was she as humble?" Asherby broke in with a snort.

"Silence!' Bugbear barked. "I have deemed you worthy of sharing a sacred memory I have revealed to none before, and I demand you show respect!"

Asherby frowned and nodded with lowered eyes.

Bugbear cleared his throat and tugged the lapels of his coat. "As I was saying, Zweenia and I shared a special bond... a desire to rediscover the ancient, lost wisdom of Non-Logical Thought, that most sacred and inscrutable school of philosophy founded by the revered goblin monk, Whittlegrip. We would spend hours in the library, delving into the musty mysteries of long untouched tomes, the sacred secrets of scattered scrolls, and the profound perplexities of priceless parchments. I dare say those were the happiest times of my mostly unhappy life. Zweenia brought out a deep, hidden facet of my personality... freeing a small, secret spot in my soul that could smile, laugh, and live. To be with her was to see the world in bright green pastures, pristine dogwood blossoms, and regal blue skies. I tell you, my friend, for all your cloddish cuddling and cooing, you humans could never know the graceful perfection of my love for Zweenia. Do you imagine your little puppy-dog droolings and ticklish tummy rubs even approach the glory and utter bliss of two magnificent minds intertwined in a journey through knowledge and discovery? Never! Never, I tell you!"

Bugbear staggered, the weight of his own words and emotions overwhelming him. Asherby rushed to steady him, but the goblin gently pushed him away.

"I am fine," he grunted. "The memory threatened to devour me for a moment. But I'm back in control." Bugbear exhaled sharply and continued. "And yet for all of this pure and glorious love I felt for Zweenia, I never told her. I never revealed the depth of my admiration, my affection, my devotion. I never told her I loved her." The goblin's lips twitched a moment, as though his heart and tongue fought a battle over what words to release next. "Then darkness fell over our little paradise. The regents at Ysgol Gwybod decided they could fatten their pockets by charging tuition fees to the students. Up to that point Ysgol Gwybod had been a free institution supported by taxes and donations. And it was no surprise that after hearing news of the new tuition many of the students were soon up in arms... Zweenia among them. Even though she was a child of privilege, she abhorred the idea that knowledge should be treated as a commodity rather than a right. She organized a protest and we marched upon the hall of regents. The regents were prepared, however, and met us with a barrage of contraband Áes dána alchemy and weapons from the ramparts above. In the chaos the protesters devolved into a stampeding mob. I was swept away with the retreating throng, losing all track of my beloved Zweenia. I fought my way back through the raging mass of goblins, using what little I knew of Non-Logical Thought at the time to bend and warp events to my will. Finally I broke through the thinning mob, only to behold the still body of my beloved." Bugbear paused, his mouth hesitant with misery, his throat thickened by grief. "There was a spark of life yet left in her as I knelt down beside her. There was still time for me to tell her how I felt. To say, *'I love you'*. But all I did was stare at her, watching the light dim in her beautiful eyes." Bugbear collapsed, kneeling on the ground, his eyes wide and unblinking. "I've never forgiven myself for not telling her. And as penance I've spoken my mind ever since, no matter the consequences."

Asherby knelt beside the goblin, placing a hand upon his shoulder. "I'm sorry."

With trembling hand Bugbear brushed Asherby away. "Don't be," he hissed. "If you say what's in your heart, you'll never be sorry. Never! So, tell Rígan how you feel. For the greatest tragedy in creation is the word unspoken."

"I barely know her," Asherby said with a shake of his head. "I wouldn't know where to start."

The goblin's face flushed orange as it filled with emotion, and his eyes grew wider still, like balloons filled to the point of bursting. "Then write it down!" Bugbear blurted as he struggled to his feet. "Just put it into words!"

Asherby nodded as he stood. "But I have to ask, why did you find me worthy of sharing your story? It's not like you to be so... emotional."

Bugbear smiled, the deep angst and misery wrought by his memories slowly evaporating. "I don't pretend to understand the human heart... or even the goblin heart. But I do know that the last time I encountered a human pining for an otherworldly beauty, their love was instrumental in destroying the Shadow Smith. Perhaps your silly sentiments will do the same in our battle against the Baymaari."

"Doubtful," Asherby said, his mouth in a half-smirk. "But I'll take your advice all the same." The tall man removed a pencil and paper from his coat pocket. "Any suggestions on where to start?"

Bugbear giggled as he waddled down the cobbled path towards the winding stream. "Start with your heart, you stupid, stupid man."

CHAPTER 22
FINAL STOP

Maga rested her head on Manchester's shoulder. Her husband slept, sputtering and snoring like an infant pig as the passenger car they rode in scuttled over the iron rails. The car rocked and puttered in a rhythmic chant and Maga found its mechanical din unsettling. In the seat across from them Riley and Tudmire slept, the patchwork's feet occasionally nudging the goblin's ribs and his tail often wagging beneath Tudmire's bulbous nose.

Maga wondered how humans could stand traveling in such a fashion, crammed into tin cans and pulled across country by smoke-belching monsters of iron. There may have been some kind of efficiency to such travel, but it denied the soul a vital connection with the earth, the air, and the sacred dance of creation.

She smiled suddenly to herself, thinking of Bugbear. How he would rage against her for letting her head fill with such saccharine syrup. And yet, she felt he would agree with her about the basic virtues of the trail over the train. A goblin such as himself who never sat still would be tormented by these confines even more than a dragon bride.

With a sigh Maga lifted her head from Manchester's shoulder and stared out the window at the black and everywhere night. Its pitch seemed to coat the world, smothering existence and snuffing out time. For all she knew they might have left reality altogether, and now traveled in some endless, empty landscape.

She turned about, looking to the back of the car. Pfeil and the other Áes dána huddled around the dim light of a will-o'-wisp, laying down wagers on a game of Noggle Stones, while Pope and his men slumped in their seats nearby, snoring and grumbling with their hats pulled down over their eyes.

The train lurched violently, sending the passengers, both slumbering and awake, spilling from their seats and onto the floor and into the aisle. Maga was able to steady herself and Manchester, but poor Tudmire and Riley fell into a confused tangle.

"What was that?" Manchester blurted, shaking the sleep from his head.

"I'll find out," Maga said, standing and awkwardly navigating her way through the swaying and rocking train car.

She opened the door near the front of the car, the night air rushing in and nearly bowling her over. But even more startling was the eerie glow that met her eyes... a luminescent rainbow painting the night and stretching out for miles across the path of the train. As she covered her eyes and squinted, Maga saw that the light was reflected off of a great wall of white crystal, nearly a mile high, that grew across the railroad tracks and to either side for as far as the eye could see.

"Stop the train!" she shouted ahead to Bixby and Cobblestone, her voice struggling to break through the clamor of the steam engine.

"What?" Bixby called back from the cab.

Maga grumbled and waved her arms. "Stop! The! Train!"

Bixby shrugged and held up the broken brake lever. "Can't!"

Maga shook her head with disbelief and retreated back inside the passenger car. "We have a problem," she said in a low whisper as she approached Manchester.

"What is it?" Manchester asked, standing up and placing his hands on her shoulders.

"There's some... thing... obstructing the tracks ahead," she answered. "And the brakes are out."

"Tudmire," Manchester whispered, "get everyone to the back of the car. Try to secure any loose baggage and rip out some of the seat cushions for padding."

The fat goblin nodded. Manchester followed Maga to the door at the front of the car. As Manchester opened the door Maga steadied the king when the wind hit them. He called ahead to Bixby and Cobblestone, waving them towards the car.

"Come back to the car! We'll disconnect it from the engine!"

"That's crazy!" Cobblestone shouted.

"It's our only chance!" Manchester called, his voice fat with irritation. He turned to Maga. "We'll need a lever or crowbar. Something to pry the coupling pin loose."

Maga nodded and darted back inside. She rushed to the back of the car where Tudmire directed the soldiers and Áes dána in tying down the luggage and equipment. "Does anyone have a pole or bar?" she asked. "We need something to pry loose the connecting pin."

Pfeil nodded, reaching into the overhead compartment and retrieving an Áes dána spear. "This work?" he said.

"Perfect!" Maga answered, taking the spear and heading back to the platform at the front of the car.

As she arrived Maga witnessed Manchester coaxing an irate Cobblestone to jump from the engine cab onto the passenger car platform. Bixby had already crossed and reached out to help the dwarf, who grumbled and waved the boy away.

"Stay back!" Cobblestone yelled. "I ain't no helpless infant!"

"Blast it!" Manchester exclaimed. "We don't have time for this!" The king stepped off the platform, his feet resting on the coupler as he reached out with one hand while holding the platform railing with the other. He plucked the dwarf up by the shirt collar and hoisted him in the air.

"Dagnabit!" the little man blurted. "Don't manhandle me!"

Manchester grunted, swung the dwarf about, and shoved him into Bixby's arms. Maga quickly helped steady the king back onto the platform. "Take the little cuss inside and keep him out of the way!" Manchester shouted to the boy.

Bixby pulled Cobblestone into the car, a string of curses trailing behind them.

Maga presented the spear. Manchester clasped his hands together and shook them, a look of relief crossing his face. He grabbed the shaft of the spear and with Maga he guided the spearhead towards the pin in the coupling that connected the car to the engine.

"Now, pry!" he ordered, his voice straining over the sound of the locomotive.

Using the railing on the platform for leverage, they pried at the pin.

"It's stuck!" Maga yelled.

"Keep trying!" Manchester exclaimed.

Suddenly Maga noticed a third set of hands prying at the shaft. She turned to see a grinning Pfeil standing behind her.

"Need help?" he asked.

"Thank you!" Maga answered with a smile.

The three of them struggled, pulling on the spear handle, straining with every muscle, exerting every iota of strength... until the pin budged.

"It's working!" Manchester called out. "Keep going!"

Then, as they set in for another pry, the train jerked as the tracks went into a turn. The spear shaft snapped where Manchester gripped it, stabbing huge splinters into his hands.

"Martin!" Maga called out as the king fell back on the platform.

Manchester held out his hands and grimaced. "Just when we had it," he sighed.

Maga looked at the wounds, dampening the blood with a handkerchief.

"Is almost loose!" Pfeil yelled as stepped off the platform onto the coupling. "Can reach pin from here!"

"Pfeil! No!" Maga called out to the Áes dána.

The big archer stretched out his hand, his fingertips nudging the top of the pin. Straining, he stepped further out onto the coupling, maintaining a precarious balance as he finally grasped the pin and removed it.

"Is done!" he called out, holding up the pin. The car slowly separated from the engine.

The voices of the king and queen broke into triumphant laughter. "Well done, Pfeil!" Maga exclaimed.

"Riley not only one who laugh at danger, eh?" the archer called back.

The joy of their success soon shattered into terror as the car went into another turn, jerking Pfeil from his perch and sending him tumbling onto the tracks.

"No!" Maga screamed as Pfeil fell from sight.

Manchester grimaced, holding her back with his wounded hands as the train car slowed and the engine sped on ahead.

Maga shook her head, blinking back tears. "He might still be alive, Martin."

"Maga," Manchester said, "wait until the car has stopped."

She frowned to him and stood. With a silent motion she swung over the railing and landed on the grass beside the tracks. The passenger car and cattle car behind it had slowed to a crawl by this point. As Maga sprinted back down the tracks, she heard Riley call after her from the back of the car.

"Where are you going?"

Maga closed her eyes, the boy's voice like a spear in her heart. "Stay put, Riley!" she called back.

She heard Riley's feet hit the gravel on the tracks, and then shortly after, his panting breath as he caught up to her.

"What is it?" he asked. "Why are you running away from the car?"

In the darkness an eerie green glow lit the tracks ahead of them. Maga felt a sudden weakness in her legs and a churning in her stomach. "Riley, go back!" she ordered.

Riley ignored her, staring with alarm at the green glow and the figure illuminated by it. "Pfeil?" he whimpered.

The young patchwork darted ahead of Maga. She reached out to him, but suddenly, overcome with grief and emotion, she fell to her knees sobbing.

"Will-o'-wisp break open when I fall," Pfeil coughed as Riley crept towards him. "Always wonder what inside them. Now know... is green snot." The big Áes dána laughed weakly.

Riley whined as he knelt at Pfeil's side. "Are you okay?"

Pfeil smiled, his eyes getting wet. "I die now, Riley."

"No," Riley sobbed. "Don't."

"Is okay," Pfeil gulped. "You are safe. Friends are safe. I do good thing." He winced as he grasped the small gold medallion that hung about his neck. "See this? I win in bogenschiessen tournament. My bogenschiessen was best." Pfeil coughed, his body trembling and convulsing. Riley lowered his muzzle onto the Áes dána's chest. Pfeil rubbed the boy's hair, smiling to him as he tore the medallion from his neck and placed it in Riley's paw. "Your bogenschiessen is best now, Riley."

In the soft green glow of the shattered will-o'-wisp, Pfeil breathed his last. Riley whined, picking up Pfeil's limp hand and placing it back on his head. As the Áes dána's lifeless hand slid back down to the ground, Riley raised his head to the sky and howled. He howled until his voice cracked and broke into a hoarse sob.

Maga, her own voice crippled by sorrow, knelt down behind Riley and held him tight. "I'm here, my boy," she whispered.

The glow from the shattered will-o'-wisp ebbed, as a mile down the tracks the steam engine plowed into the crystal wall, the explosion sending tremors through the ground, and a great ball of fire erupting up into the night sky.

Riley turned to Maga, burying his tear-drenched muzzle into her shoulder. "Why?" he cried. "Our parents. Mother Twitchett. Pfeil. Why, Maga?'

"I don't know," Maga said between sobs. "But I do know you were special to all of them." She paused, holding the young patchwork tighter. "And you're special to me too."

"Don't leave us, Maga," Riley pleaded, his voice thin and weak.

"I'll never leave my little prince," Maga promised, running her fingers through his thick fur and kissing the top of his head. "Never."

Bugbear found the tylluan flight rather disappointing. Being nighttime, there was little opportunity for sightseeing. Plus, the force of the wind made it impossible to get any reading done. And Threelgon, while as proficient a rider as he had boasted, proved a poor traveling companion. He had ignored every one of Bugbear's attempts to initiate a sing-a-long. The goblin had even dusted off a few old Áes dána ditties in the hopes of stirring his dour pilot into some kind of camaraderie. And yet, the unseelie warrior remained silent, his one good eye set on the horizon and his hands firmly on the reins.

Bugbear glanced over to Rígan and Asherby, smiling as the tall man regaled the laughing queen with some long, rambling reminiscence of his adventures in Washington society. A few wing beats behind them, Brenen rode with another tylluan pilot. Even the lowly owl-keeper seemed to find some connection with his companion, sharing a few chuckle-inducing jokes and limericks.

"You are in for a treat!" Bugbear piped to Threelgon, deciding one last time to try to entice his one-eyed guide into socializing. "Washington has electric power. I imagine the lights will be quite a spectacle from up here."

"I can see them already," Threelgon answered, pointing to an eerie, luminous rainbow breaking over the horizon.

Bugbear peered around Threelgon, his wide eyes widening more as he witnessed the uncanny aura, its height reaching miles into the pitch black sky and its breadth stretching across the entirety of the horizon. "That's a Bilröst barrier!" Bugbear exclaimed.

"Impossible!" Threelgon snorted. "I've never seen one that big before!"

"I know Áes dána alchemy when I see it," Bugbear replied. "That aura is the mystical runoff from Bilröst crystal. The Áes dána have laid siege to Washington, D.C.!"

"Let's take a closer look," Threelgon said, motioning to Rígan and the other tylluan rider to descend towards the phenomenon.

As the tylluans skimmed through the mysterious lights, Bugbear could see the mile high, white crystal wall below. Like broken bones jutting through a dead man's skin, the giant crystal shards protruded through the earth, overlapping each other and forming an impenetrable barrier. Below Bugbear noticed a fire at the base of the wall, and in its illumination he saw railroad tracks and some obscure movement. People perhaps?

They flew beyond the oppressive expanse of the Bilröst barrier and over the defeated city of Washington, its great lights dimmed by despair and its vitality smothered by occupation. Bugbear noticed small campfires and the occasional will-o'-wisp winking from below, the greatest concentration of activity seeming to center around Capitol Hill.

"Can you get in closer?" Bugbear asked Threelgon, pointing to the Capitol Building, its marble facade illuminated by several large bonfires on the front lawn.

Threelgon nodded and guided the tylluan down towards the gathering. As they drew closer, Bugbear's keen goblin ears picked up a low murmur... a deep, rumbling mantra mouthed by the multitudes below.

"Durm taln nawneev larnawl kir har anduv durm."

"Pull up, Threelgon!" Bugbear panicked. "Pull up!"

A banshee ball screamed towards them, its eerie tail of green fire like a leash broke loose from the Devil's hand. Threelgon quickly steered the tylluan to the left, unsettling Bugbear from his place on the saddle. The goblin tumbled from the owl, only spared from a fatal fall by Threelgon's quick grab for his coat collar. The rider's attention now distracted from guiding the tylluan, the banshee ball clipped its wing, crippling the mighty raptor and sending it spinning towards the ground. Bugbear swung from Threelgon's grasp and took hold of the leather saddle strap about the owl's belly.

"Don't mind me!" the goblin called up. "Just bring this beast in for a safe landing!"

Threelgon gritted his teeth and pulled on the reins, trying to coax the tylluan up from its nosedive.

Rígan pulled her owl up beside them. "Try to guide it over the wall!" she called to Threelgon. She swerved her mount to avoid another banshee ball that screamed between them. Fortunately Asherby seemed to have had a better hold on her than Bugbear had on Threelgon. "We'll meet you over there!"

Rígan and the other pilot peeled off as Threelgon continued to struggle with his wounded owl. Bugbear dangled from the strap, his eyes filled with dread as he gazed down at the multitude of Baymaari infected warriors, all of them chanting their bitter, sinister oath.

"Mind your legs!" Threelgon yelled to Bugbear.

The goblin looked up to see the crystal wall looming before him. He pulled himself up, hugging the underside of the owl like a tick. Bugbear felt the razor tip of one of the crystals rip the tail of his coat as Threelgon guided the tylluan over the wall.

"I can't keep him in the air any longer!" Threelgon shouted. "Get ready to jump!"

Bugbear breathed deeply, watching the ground get closer and closer. He now saw the source of the fire he had seen earlier... a locomotive had hit the wall. A horrible way to travel anyway, he thought to himself.

"Jump!" Threelgon ordered as they glided in at about 15 feet above the ground.

Bugbear dropped from the belly of the tylluan, closing his eyes and bracing for a bone-shattering impact. Instead he was met with the supple and forgiving embrace of canvas. Confused and bewildered, he opened his eyes and looked about. Several United States soldiers held a tarp stretched between them, Bugbear safely caught in the center. To the side the goblin could see two train cars stalled on the tracks, and a group of Áes dána dignitaries and soldiers unloading horses and other gear.

"This belong to you?" one of the soldiers holding the tarp called to a figure hidden in shadows.

A tall man strode from behind, the early dawn light slowly revealing a very familiar bearded face and top hat.

"Manchester?" Bugbear said in amazement and joy.

There were hugs, first of all... hugs and such a jumble of emotion and relief that no single person dominated the moment. Bugbear hugged Manchester. Maga hugged Bugbear. Tudmire hugged Bugbear. Asherby hugged Rígan... which, while seeming quite odd and inappropriate to Rígan at the time, she nevertheless found quite pleasant.

Bugbear also offered young Riley condolences for the loss of his mentor. Although the goblin had never met Pfeil, he could tell by the way Riley spoke of him that the archer possessed superior character and temperament when compared to the typical Áes dána.

"His sacrifice shall not be forgotten any time soon," Bugbear promised the young patchwork.

Riley appreciated this sentiment, all the more in knowing Bugbear's discomfort and distaste in dealing with such emotional situations.

Introductions were made as well, and Manchester found the unseelie travelers, with their rough yet direct and honest manner, a far more palatable sort than their Áes dána kin. Asherby as well ingratiated himself with the king and queen, his diplomacy and demeanor a shade cooler than Pope and his men.

Bugbear was particularly fascinated with the Dabblers. He spent a considerable amount of time enquiring about their order, their inventions, and their intentions. While Bixby was happy to divulge the information, Cobblestone remained stubborn and insistent in his guarding of the Dabbler's secrets.

"Blast an' blarney!" the dwarf cursed. "You gonna tell our secrets t'every stray varmint what's got a tongue t'ask?"

Bugbear assured the dwarf that he would keep their enigmas

sufficiently guarded, and promised to reveal a few secrets of his own later on.

Threelgon also bid farewell to Luther, his loyal tylluan. The banshee ball had done too much damage to the wing, and it would have been a great cruelty to keep Luther alive. With a swift jab of his sword to the owl's spine, he rid the creature of its suffering. As was the custom of the unseelie, he left the carcass for the carrion eaters.

After gathering their supplies and mounts from the train cars, the haphazard collection of refugees and adventurers made camp in an abandoned barn roughly a half mile south of the railroad tracks. Here Maga bandaged Manchester's wounds, the Áes dána made preparations for Pfeil's burial, and Bugbear reported his discoveries to the king and queen.

"I fear what began as a few isolated incidents has grown into a full-fledged Baymaari epidemic," Bugbear said as he examined Manchester's maps of Washington, D.C. "The Áes dána in particular seem to have been targeted. I'm guessing it may have something to do with their longtime use of Coranieid rooted alchemy. The telltale Coranieid stench probably attracted the Baymaari... like crows to carrion."

"Speaking of the Coranieid," Manchester said, flexing his newly bandaged hands, "we learned that Ollamh Cron is alive, and continuing her experiments."

"Extraordinary!" Bugbear exclaimed. "I had a very disturbing encounter with Duergar at the Unseelie Court as well. It seems the Baymaari have resurrected some generals for their army... a kind of *Culst Mardarri*, or *Thinking Dead*."

"Do you think the Smith will return as well?" Maga asked.

"No," Bugbear said with a shake of the head and a wave of the hand. "The Smith has already played the game and he lost. He wouldn't be able to play again while a new player is setting up the board for a new game. But his old pawns can and are being used by the Baymaari."

"Well, their everyday foot soldiers seem to be as allergic to hope as the Shadow Smith was," Maga added. "At least that's what we discovered in our encounter with them."

"As did we," Bugbear said as he circled an area of the map with his pen. "But judging by the size of the force I saw at the Capitol steps, a few simple phrases and symbols won't disperse this threat. It will take something massive and bold."

"What do you have in mind?" Manchester asked.

"I'm not sure yet," Bugbear said stroking his chin and eying Bixby and Cobblestone as they quarreled in a far corner over the pieces of their mechanical maiden. "But something will come to me."

"Cousin!" Tudmire shouted as he waddled up to Bugbear with a steaming bowl of stew in his hands. "I don't imagine that unseelie fare was very filling, so I saved an extra helping of hobnob stew for you."

"Ah, dear Tudmire!" Bugbear exclaimed, receiving the bowl with a smile. "How I've missed your cooking!" The goblin leaned over to Manchester, his voice low and secretive. "You hid the pepper from him, right?"

Manchester nodded, stifling a chortle.

"And hobnob stew is one of my favorites!" Bugbear smiled as he turned back to Tudmire.

"Eat up!" Tudmire piped. And then he turned about to tend to the big pot boiling on the campfire outside the barn.

Bugbear spooned a helping of stew into his mouth, closing his eyes and grinning. "First time I've ever eaten his cooking without sneezing." He offered the bowl up to Manchester and Maga. "Care for a bite?"

Maga turned away, covering her mouth and gasping.

"Hmmm," Bugbear mused. "Pregnant." And then the goblin shoveled another spoonful of stew into his mouth.

"Excuse me?" Manchester blurted.

Maga turned back to the goblin, her face painted white with panic.

"Well, it's obvious, isn't it?" Bugbear snickered. "There's the nausea. There's the maternal glow. There's the considerable weight gain."

"I have not gained weight, you little pumpkin-headed heathen!" Maga fumed.

"There's the mood swings," Bugbear shrugged, slurping up another mouthful of stew.

Manchester took Maga's hands as joy exploded across his face. "Is it true?" he asked.

Maga's head shook and nodded and shrugged. "It could be," she whispered. "But no dragon bride has ever been with child. Not since my mother died."

"Trust me," Bugbear said, waving his spoon at them. "Pregnant. Congratulations."

Sudden shouts and outrage bubbled outside the barn. Bugbear grumbled and set his bowl of stew on the ground as he heard Brenen and the Áes dána refugees exchanging bitter accusations. He stood up and pulled on his tattered coat-of-many-pockets, nodding to Manchester and Maga.

"It seems dinner defers to diplomacy," the goblin said, bowing and motioning the king and queen ahead.

Outside the barn the Áes dána stood in a cluster near a freshly dug grave, their banners and flags pitched in the nearby dirt. Riley stood near them, eying Pfeil's shrouded body with discomfort. Brenen, Threelgon, Asherby, and Rígan stood across from the Áes dána, their bodies animated by frustration and conflict.

"But I am the official who sponsored Pfeil's transfer to our kingdom," Brenen argued before the cluster of Áes dána chieftains. "Áes dána law requires I attend the funeral."

"No!" one of the chieftains spat. "We have disrupted tradition enough already by allowing Pfeil's patchwork friend to attend. To allow an unseelie to be there as well...?"

"My condition does not affect my ability to perform my familial duties!" Brenen replied. "I will step down from my position as king without incident. But I am honor bound to pay last respects to my cousin."

"If you truly cared about honor," one of the other chieftains snorted, "you would have killed yourself rather than be seen in such a disgraceful state."

Brenen opened his mouth to protest, but shame and anguish weighed down his tongue and his gaze.

Threelgon stepped forward, his hand on his sword hilt. "Unseelie ranks have been a bit thin of late," he growled. "Perhaps I should start a recruitment drive."

Brenen waved the one-eyed warrior down. "What does it matter?" he muttered. "Pfeil wouldn't have wanted an owl-keeper at his funeral."

"Now you speak sense," a chieftain grinned.

"A moment, if you please," Tudmire said, waddling over from the campfire and waving his hand to the chieftains.

"Tudmire," Bugbear whispered. "This is Áes dána business. Best to stay out of such tangled bureaucracy."

"Tut-tut, cousin," Tudmire answered. "They haven't invented a bureaucracy that can out-tangle me." The fat goblin strolled between the unseelie and the Áes dána, tugging at his suspenders and smacking his lips. "I seem to recall a wager betwixt you Áes dána folk and myself."

"Well, yes," one of the chieftains answered with a nod.

"And I won that wager, did I not?"

"Yes."

"And the conditions of that wager were that you Áes dána remain silent until we reach Washington, D.C. Is that not correct?"

"That is correct," the Áes dána replied with a snarl.

Tudmire motioned to the large crystal wall that obscured and dominated everything to the east. "Washington, D.C. lies on the other side of that lovely Áes dána barrier," the goblin said. "Which means, you lot need to shut your bloody pieholes!"

Bugbear laughed and clapped his hands. "Well played, cousin!"

The Áes dána fumed and grumbled, but clenched their mouths shut.

Rígan stepped forward. "That means that Brenen, being the only other person here who knows the complete Rites of Oberon, must attend the ceremony."

Brenen offered a small smile of gratitude to Rígan. She returned the smile and gave him a quick, affectionate rub to the back of his neck. The chieftain frowned and waved Brenen over to the graveside.

"Well," Tudmire sighed with satisfaction, "now I can cook in peace while Pfeil rests in peace." The fat seneschal returned to the bubbling stew, dipping in a pinky and licking it with a contented hum.

As the mourners laid Pfeil to rest, Bugbear, Manchester, Maga, Asherby, Rígan, and Threelgon moved back towards the barn for privacy.

"The king, queen, and I have exchanged information," Bugbear whispered to the impromptu council. "We're quite certain that we face a Baymaari invasion on the other side of that wall. The real unknown is the status of the American forces."

"Most of the troops would have fallen back to protect the President at the White House," Asherby offered.

"Good luck getting there," Threelgon said. "Even if you could get through the Bilröst barrier, there are still thousands of Baymaari drones to get past."

"Washington is honeycombed with secret underground tunnels," Asherby said. "There's an entrance at Senator McComas' carriage house, 'bout two miles south of here."

"On our side of the barrier?" Manchester asked.

Asherby nodded.

"I'll come with you," Manchester said.

"And me," Maga added.

Manchester shook his head. "Not in your condition."

"We don't even know for certain that I'm pregnant," Maga argued.

"Yes you do," Bugbear interrupted. "Trust me. Pregnant. Congratulations."

"Oh, congratulations!" Rígan fussed.

"Wonderful," Asherby said with a smile. "Congratulations. Nice to have some pleasant news for a change."

"Yes," Manchester nodded and smiled. "And what would be even more pleasant is if the mother-to-be would remain here where it's safe."

"Regardless of my condition, I have more battle experience than anyone else here," Maga said firmly.

"I've been in the army for 15 years," Asherby offered, holding up his hand.

"I've been at this for 75 years," Maga smirked.

Manchester cocked his head and looked to Maga with a single upraised eyebrow. "Exactly how old are you?"

"If anyone makes any more comments about my age or weight...!" Maga blustered.

"Like I said, moody," Bugbear whispered to Manchester.

"Listen," Asherby said, with a diffusing tone, "the mission may sound more dangerous than it actually is. The existence of these tunnels is classified information. Only a select few authorized personnel even know where they are and how to access them. So it's not likely any of these zombies is going to have the knowledge it would take to uncover them. I'm nearly 100 percent certain we won't run into any threats."

"*Nearly 100 percent*?" Manchester frowned.

"Well," Asherby replied, "I can't promise a few lobbyist couldn't have found their way down there. This is Washington, after all."

"If it will make you feel better," Maga said, placing a hand on Manchester's shoulder, "invite Pope and a few of his men along too. We'll still be traveling light, but we'll have some backup in case we get into trouble."

"I suppose," Manchester said with a sour expression. The king turned to Bugbear. "As for the Baymaari, has that *something* come to you yet?"

The goblin did not hear Manchester. His eyes were fixed on Rígan, piercing her with a long, semi-conscious stare. The unseelie queen looked to him quizzically as she shifted in place with discomfort.

"Bugbear?" Manchester nudged the goblin.

"Yes," Bugbear hissed.

"Can you hear me?"

"Yes," the goblin hissed louder, turning from Rígan and staring at the Dabblers as they argued in the far corner of the barn.

"Do you have a plan for dealing with the Baymaari?" Manchester asked his advisor.

Bugbear's gaze shifted over to Brenen at the graveside service several paces away. "Yes!" the goblin suddenly exclaimed.

"Care to share it with us?" Maga asked, her brow raised in a mix of amusement and confusion.

"No!" the goblin laughed as he suddenly broke from his trance and danced away from the group.

Asherby sighed and slapped Manchester on the shoulder as they watched Bugbear stumble towards the Dabblers. "Yeah. It'll be nice being around humans again."

Thick soot coated the ground and the walls of the tunnels, and overhead the support beams were charred black and gray. Manchester bent down to poke at a discarded musket, its wooden stock all black and rotting and its metal barrel all rusted and crumbling.

"Maid doesn't get down here often, I take it?" the king said to Asherby.

"This is from an old fire," Riley said as he sniffed at the ground. The patchwork lifted his head, nose twitching in the light breeze that snaked through the tunnel. "It died long before any of us were born."

"The boy has a nose for history," Asherby smirked. "Happened back when the British invaded Washington during the War of 1812," he elaborated as he patted one of the timber beams, knocking loose a small cloud of black dust. "No structural damage. It's perfectly safe."

A large chunk of rock dislodged from the ceiling and splintered as it hit the ground in front of the party of explorers.

"Safe as long as you stop touching things," Maga said with a sideways glance to Asherby.

The tall man shrugged and offered the queen a sheepish grin. "My apologies, ma'am." He gave a slight bow and stepped in front of the group, holding the electric lantern the Dabblers had provided, and continuing to guide the expedition through the tunnels beneath Washington, D.C.

"He seems a bit... distracted," Maga whispered to Manchester as they crept through the dark passageway.

"I know that look on his face," Manchester grinned as he gripped Maga's hand tightly. "Used to stare back at me every day in the mirror around the time I first met you."

Maga elbowed the king and smiled brightly. "Think he fancies Rígan?"

"I was going to suggest Cobblestone," Manchester snorted. "But I suppose Rígan is the more practical choice, since he's known her longer."

Maga laughed, a sound Manchester never tired of hearing. Soon that laughter would be doubled. They would welcome a child into the world... an heir to the throne.

The king turned as he heard scuffling and mirth behind them. He watched with annoyance as Riley scurried after a rat, zigzagging across the tunnels with wild enthusiasm. Pope and his men chuckled at the patchwork's antics, and Manchester could tell Riley's fumbles and stumbles were mostly a show for the soldiers. The rat scampered into a hole in the tunnel wall, and Riley barked after it, shoving his snout into the gap and wagging his behind with exaggerated outrage.

Pope snickered as he bent down behind the patchwork and held out his hand. "Is he allowed to have peppermint?" the lieutenant asked Manchester as he reached into his coat pocket.

Manchester nodded with a friendly grin.

Riley turned from his erstwhile prey and trotted over to Pope to receive the treat. "Good lad," Pope said, patting him on the head.

"I don't think we should have let Riley come along," Manchester sighed, turning back to Maga.

"I couldn't leave him behind," Maga whispered, lowering her eyes. "Not after what he just went through with Pfeil."

"He's just a boy," Manchester exhaled. "We've already asked him to endure so much. I mean, how many other boys his age have battled madmen and zombies?"

"I want to adopt him," Maga said suddenly, turning to

Manchester with soft, wet eyes.

"What?" Manchester blurted. Then with a quick discretionary stoop he leaned in to whisper. "We have a child of our own on the way."

"All the better," Maga said, her smile deflecting the tears around her cheeks. "Our baby will have a loyal and loving elder brother waiting."

"But we're already Riley's guardians," Manchester argued, even as her words had begun to wear away at his resistance.

"You yourself said the he deserves parents," Maga said. "I want to be his mother. I love him that much, Martin."

"I love him too, Maga," Manchester replied, his own voice cracking with heavy emotion. "Mother Twitchett always did say how special he was."

"He deserves this," Maga sighed, biting her lower lip. "*We* deserve this."

Manchester squeezed her hand. "I'll have Tudmire draw up the papers when we get back to Willow Prairie."

Maga squeezed Manchester's hand in return, and bent in to softly kiss him on the lips. "You'll make a wonderful father."

"Pappy," Manchester said with a firm nod.

"What?" Maga chuckled.

"That's what I want to be called," Manchester winked to her. "Pappy."

Asherby's lantern shattered against the tunnel wall and the hum of the electric light fizzled, sputtered, and died. The government agent cried out briefly before he fell back as though kicked by a steam-powered mule. Manchester caught him, although the force of the impact nearly sent him tumbling as well.

"What is it?" Manchester asked Maga, his eyes adjusting to the gloom of the tunnels.

Maga peered ahead, her silver eyes flashing like diamond orbs. "Baymaari," she gasped, drawing her sword and moving in front of Manchester and Asherby.

Manchester grumbled as he roughly helped Asherby to his feet. "One of your lobbyist?" he said, drawing his twelve-shooters. "Someone light a lantern!" he called back to Pope and his men. The king blindly stepped forward, calling to his wife in the hopes she had not wandered too far ahead. "Maga, come back here!" He sighed as he heard her sword singing several paces before him, her warrior's impulse not yet reined in by her maternal instincts.

In the darkness the Baymaari host moaned their eerie chorus... *"Durm taln nawneev larnawl kir har anduv durm."* Pope fumbled with his flint and steel, finally igniting the lantern wick. He passed it up to Asherby who held it up in front of Manchester. The orange and yellow light washed the darkness away, illuminating a semi circle of tunnel ahead of them. Manchester could now see his wife, swinging and slashing her sword against the enemy like an artist smearing and spreading her brush over a canvas. Manchester never thought violence could look so elegant. And yet, it was the enemy itself that caused Manchester the greater alarm. Maga faced a swarm of dull-eyed United States soldiers, each of them muttering the bone-chilling dirge as they swung their clumsy weapons. Some of them wore Civil War era uniforms, while others wore the garb of western cavalry soldiers. Still others were nothing more than shambling bones in tattered rags.

"I'd forgotten," Asherby frowned. "This tunnel runs beneath the National Cemetery."

"That information would have been useful earlier," Manchester growled. "Maga!" the king called ahead, trying to shout over the growing hum of the Baymaari chant. "Move aside! Let me get a clear shot!"

"What does it matter?" Maga shouted back, her sword skewering one of the undead creatures. The demon hissed at the dragon bride and pulled itself down the blade towards her, rifle butt raised to strike. Maga kicked the creature back, sending it tumbling into its fellows. "It's just like at the Nagonene burial mound! They won't stay down!"

"Then fall back!" Manchester shouted. "We'll stop them the same way!" Manchester quickly holstered his pistols and reached into his vest pocket. He removed his royal quill and turned back to Asherby, Pope, and the others. "Does anyone have any paper?"

The confused soldiers patted their pockets and packs. Asherby hesitantly removed a folded paper from his inside coat pocket, handing it to Manchester. "Just a letter I was writing," he muttered.

Manchester received the paper and unfolded it. "There's already writing on it," he grumbled. "I need a blank paper or something that's...." Manchester stopped as he glanced at the letter. *"My dearest Rígon...?"* he read aloud.

Asherby snatched the letter back as he glowered at Manchester. "We're soldiers, I'm afraid," he said as he placed the letter back in his pocket. "Most of us are only going to have official documents or identification papers."

"Or budding love letters," Manchester snorted as he returned the quill to his pocket.

"We'll have to retreat," Maga said as she backed into the conversation, her sword held before her in an attempt to keep the advancing Baymaari at bay.

A pistol fired and a bullet ricocheted off the tunnel wall, careening into an undead soldier's back. The creature trembled a moment, its mouth stretching open and dark gray ash spewing up from its gullet. It fell limp and collapsed to the ground in an unmoving heap.

Manchester looked back at Pope and his men, but saw them huddling in the dark, as confused and uncertain about the source of the discharge as he was.

Another pistol, then a rifle, then two pistols… soon the tunnels echoed with gunfire, and the Baymaari fell with each bullet that pierced their dead flesh and shattered their lifeless bones. The tunnels swarmed with thick clouds of gray as bubbles of dirt and dust vomited from the inert corpses. Manchester, Maga, and Asherby fell back, crouching with the rest of the group and watching the disturbing display unfold before them in the flickering lantern light. The chanting ceased as the gunfire sputtered to a few sporadic shots. The gray mist hung in the air, mixing with gun smoke and dust motes before dispersing with a soft and unearthly wail.

Manchester, Maga, and Asherby stood, looking with disbelief at the piles of corpses before them. Through the thick smoke, shadows stirred, moving over the bodies and towards the party. Maga held up her sword, while Manchester and the soldiers drew their pistols and rifles. A group of 20 armed men stepped into the lantern light before them. At the lead stood a broad-shouldered and well-dressed man with round spectacles… and beneath those spectacles twitched a nose like an owl's beak… and beneath that nose grew a mustache thick as a horse brush… and beneath that mustache gleamed teeth like square pearls. The man holstered his .38 Colt pistol and offered a brief bow to Manchester, Maga, and their party.

"Welcome to the second American Revolution," he said. "I'm Theodore Roosevelt."

CHAPTER 26
ARMED AND READY

"No!" Cobblestone shouted, waving Bugbear away from the collection of mechanical body parts. "How many times I got to tell you, we ain't letting you mutilate Matilda!"

"Matilda?" Bixby asked, raising an eyebrow. "When'd we agree to call her Matilda?"

"When I agreed not to bust you 'side the head!" Cobblestone grumbled, shaking a big wrench at his partner.

Bugbear took in a deep breath, glancing out the barn door to the field beyond where Brenen, Threelgon, and Rígan tended to the two surviving tylluans. The skies had begun to darken with rain clouds, painting the landscape in dull, gray misery. The goblin exhaled as he turned back to the Dabblers, his jaw set firm with determination.

"What are you going to use for a power source?" Bugbear asked.

Cobblestone scratched his rear with the edge of the wrench and ground his teeth in contemplation. "Ain't sussed that out yet," he muttered in defeat.

"We thought about steam," Bixby offered. "But we'd have to be shovin' coal down her throat non-stop to keep her goin'."

"And we'd have to put an exhaust pipe somewhere," the dwarf added. "Lady with smoke shootin' out her backside ain't the most stylish of company."

"I know exactly how you can empower your lady," Bugbear smiled with devious charm. "No coal. No smoke. A quiet, clean, and elegant solution."

Cobblestone lowered his arm, letting the wrench rest on the ground as his bushy eyebrows frowned. "Ain't possible."

Bugbear held up a finger and smiled. He reached into one of his coat pockets, removing two small metal wheels, about an inch in diameter, mounted on pencil-sized sticks. He then produced two small, black rectangles. He placed each of the rectangles onto each of the wheels and held them up to the Dabblers. "Being men of learning, you are familiar with the laws of magnetism, I am sure," the goblin nodded.

"Course we are!" Cobblestone blustered, nudging Bixby.

"Uhm, yeah," Bixby shrugged. "Course we are."

"Then you realize," Bugbear continued, "that like charges repel each other. Observe." Bugbear slowly drew the wheels together, and as the small rectangles came closer they trembled and moved away from each other. And as the tiny magnets repelled, they turned the wheels. And as the wheels spun around again, the magnets met and continued pushing against each other, sending the wheels on another rotation. "Perpetual motion, gentlemen."

Cobblestone dropped his wrench and dropped his jaw. "How...?"

"When we return to Willow Prairie I shall talk to the king about providing you with magnets of a sufficient size to power your lady," Bugbear said, his eyes narrowed by arrogance. "I fear this particular engine, however, is only large enough to power... oh, let's say... an arm?"

"Give it to him," Bixby sighed as he nudged the dwarf.

Cobblestone eyed Bugbear with a cross between respect and mistrust. He turned to rummage through the pile of metal body parts and roughly pulled a left arm from the mix.

"I need the right arm," Bugbear said with a shake of his head.

The dwarf grumbled and fumed as he dropped the arm to the ground and dug through the remaining parts until removing the right arm. "Here!" he grunted as he shoved the limb towards Bugbear.

The goblin took the arm and nodded as he examined it.

"Excellent craftsmanship," he said with admiration. "The seams and joints are incredibly subtle... nearly invisible." Bugbear waved the artificial hand to Cobblestone and Bixby. "Perfect for my purposes, gentlemen. You have my gratitude, and perhaps soon the gratitude of the entire world."

The dwarf and boy watched after the goblin as he waddled and out into the misty rain, carefully inserting the perpetual motion engine into the shoulder joint of the arm.

Rígan, Threelgon, and Brenen were just starting to lead the tylluans out of the rain and towards the barn when Bugbear waved them to a stop with the arm.

"Step aside, goblin," Threelgon ordered. "A storm is brewing. We need to get to shelter."

"I must have words with Rígan," Bugbear replied.

Rígan eyed Bugbear and the mechanical arm with curiosity and concern. "Go ahead without me," she said to Threelgon.

Thunder rumbled in the distance and the clouds lit with flashes of electric unrest. Threelgon exhaled sharply, gave Bugbear a bitter glance, and tugged at the reins of the tylluan as he trudged towards the barn. Brenen followed with the other owl, ducking his head into his shoulders to brace against the increasing rain shower.

Rígan pulled her hood over her head and looked to Bugbear with azure eyes, piercing and brilliant in contrast with the dull, gray sky. "What is this, little man?" she asked, nodding towards the silver arm.

"It's hope," Bugbear piped. "Your path back to the Áes dána throne."

Rígan shook her head vigorously, closing her eyes and snarling with disdain. "No. Even if what you said was possible, I would not trade my unseelie kin for the false glory and empty ritual of the

Empire."

"But the Empire was different when you were High Queen," Bugbear argued, ignoring the downpour. "You made changes. You implemented policies and legislation that ushered in an era of prosperity and peace the Áes dána had not seen since the time of Danu herself."

Rígan lowered her head, the edges of the hood hiding her pain. "And that's why they got rid of me."

"Brenen and his conspirators," Bugbear added.

"No," Rígan shook her head. "Brenen wasn't involved. He was their puppet on the throne after they eliminated me. But he had nothing to do with my accident."

"Puppet or not," Bugbear continued, "the Empire shattered after you left. But you could reunite them again. You could even bring the unseelie back into the fold."

"You think the unseelie would be better off in the tender luxuries of Áes dána civilization?" Rígan laughed.

"No!" Bugbear blurted, frustration scraping against his throat. "Let them stay in the forests! Let them remain as rough and wild as they wish to be! But at least give them a choice! Give them the opportunity to be more than warnings and ghost stories Áes dána aristocrats tell their children at night! Give them back their dignity!"

Rígan raised her head and looked to Bugbear. Thunder rumbled beneath their feet and lightning flashed in the distance. "It's not a real arm," she said. "They still wouldn't accept me."

"They would if your claim to the throne was backed by the Draíocht Ridire," Bugbear said.

Rígan arched a brow. "Would he?"

Bugbear nodded, his mouth curled by a canny smile. "Once the truth is revealed to him, he will."

Rígan lowered her hood, the rain running down her face as she stared at Bugbear with tired eyes. "How does it work?" she asked.

"I'll warn you," Bugbear started as he moved towards her with the arm, "it will be quite painful at first."

Rígan nodded, brushing the cloak off her right shoulder and rolling up the sleeve of her gown. Bugbear eased the silver arm up into the sleeve until it hit the stump at Rígan's shoulder.

"Hold it in place," Bugbear said, guiding her left arm over to grasp the silver arm.

"Shouldn't we be doing this inside out of the rain," Rígan asked.

The lightning arched behind them as a bee buzzed around Bugbear's head. "Miracles work best outside." The goblin smiled to the bee and nodded it towards Rígan. "Don't be nervous. My friend won't hurt you."

"That's nice to know," Rígan said as her eyes nervously followed the insect swarming about her head.

"Actually, I was speaking to the bee," Bugbear smirked. The goblin walked around Rígan, his eyes glancing up and down. "Remain perfectly still," he said. "Feel the beat of your heart. Feel the warm air in your lungs. The electricity flowing through your nerves."

Rígan closed her eyes and trembled slightly as a thunderbolt struck the earth roughly a half mile from where they stood.

"Open your eyes," Bugbear ordered, still circling her, still watching intently. "Look at the bee. Feel the rotation of its wings. Let your mind follow. Rotating, slowly. Turning and changing. Feel reality slip away. Feel the world dissolve." The goblin quickened his pace as he circled the unseelie queen. "There are four basic precepts of Non-Logical Thought, which can never be repeated enough. *Number one: Reality is Thought. Number two: Logic restricts*

Thought and thus restricts Reality. Number three: Abandon Logic, abandon restriction. And number four: Unrestricted Thought equals unrestricted Reality!"

Rígan's face went blank, her eyes glazing over as the bee circled her head.

Another lightning bolt hit the ground, just yards from where they stood. This time Rígan remained still and unmoving, watching the bee swarm her head as she held the silver arm to her shoulder.

Threelgon called from the barn. "Goblin! Enough of your games! Bring Rígan in here at once!"

"Tudmire!" Bugbear barked back to the barn. "Keep that one-eyed watchdog away from us!"

Threelgon roared out of the barn, sprinting towards Bugbear and Rígan.

"I suspect this will hurt me more than it will hurt you," Tudmire grunted as he scurried after Threelgon, throwing himself at the unseelie warrior's feet and wrapping his arms about his ankles. Tudmire's bulk upset the enraged warrior's balance and sent him tumbling to the muddy ground.

Bugbear turned his attention back to Rígan. "The energy that flows through you flows through your new arm," he droned. "Wires become nerves. Pistons become muscle. Tubes become veins. There is no difference. There is only life!"

The lightning struck Rígan, bathing her in white, yellow, and blue. She jerked and spasmed, her mouth opening in an anguished scream. Bugbear fell to the ground several feet away, the thunderclap sending out shockwaves that shattered his balance and scrambled his senses.

Threelgon reached out to his queen and sister, struggling to get to his feet in the slick mud. "Rígan!" he cried.

Electricity skittered across Rígan's body, drenching her in an eerie glow as she collapsed to her knees and lowered her head to the ground. The bee swarmed about her a moment longer before darting off through the rain and disappearing into the gray gloom.

Threelgon extracted himself from Tudmire's grasp and charged towards Bugbear, his desperate and determined footfalls slipping and sliding in the rain-drenched earth. He pulled the still stunned goblin up from the ground and shook him like a rag doll. "What have you done?" he growled.

Rígan trembled and sobbed as she raised her head from the mud. "Threelgon," she wept. "Let him go." The silver hand clawed into the thick mud. Rígan lifted the hand, letting the wet earth fall through the fingers. She laughed, tears rolling down her cheeks, mixing with the rain and mud. She rubbed the silver fingertips together and turned to Threelgon and Bugbear with a bright smile. "I can feel," she gasped. Trembling, Rígan lifted the silver hand to her face and wiped away the tears. "I can touch." She stood and held her arms open, lifting her face to the weeping heavens. "I am whole."

"I can feel. I can touch. I am whole."

Threelgon dropped Bugbear, letting the goblin tumble into the thick mud. The warrior's single eye welled with emotion as he gazed at his reborn queen. "It's a miracle," he gasped.

Bugbear grumbled and wallowed in the mud before pulling himself to his feet. "Yes," he said. "One of several miracles I have planned for today." The goblin trudged through the mud towards the barn. "Saddle the tylluans, Brenen," he ordered the flabbergasted former king. "The queen must address her subjects."

"And for my money, you won't find better table fare than Michigan river trout," Vice President Roosevelt said as he led Manchester's party through the winding tunnels beneath Washington.

"Indiana blue gill is better," Riley said as he tugged at the Vice President's jacket.

"Riley!" Manchester said in a stern tone. "Don't argue with the Vice President."

"Nonsense!" Roosevelt laughed. "The boy is entitled to his opinion." Roosevelt looked down to Riley and patted his head. "I imagine with that nose of yours you're a crackerjack hunter, eh?"

"We have nearly rid Willow Prairie of all the pouch-bellies and ring-tails," Riley boasted.

"Good lad!" Roosevelt laughed.

The group came to a large open area in the tunnels... a chamber where the revolutionaries were storing supplies and ammunition. Several wounded men lay on bedrolls, while others cleaned their rifles and sharpened their bayonets. A pot of coffee boiled on a small fire, and a page quickly rushed up to the Vice President with a steaming cup.

"Thank you, Franklin," Roosevelt said with a nod. The Vice President squatted on a crate and motioned for Maga, Manchester, and Asherby to do likewise. "Sit," he said. "I suspect you have as many questions for me as I have for you."

"How long has the city been under siege, Mister Vice President?" Maga asked.

"It started slowly," Roosevelt answered, his voice and face turning serious. "I suspect it began when the President was shot a few months ago. Some maniac spouting gibberish assaulted him outside of the Capitol Building. William survived, barely. But he was a changed man after that."

"How so?" Manchester asked.

"He seemed distracted," Roosevelt said, his eyes downcast as he took a sip of coffee. "Almost as if he was dreaming while awake. While he engaged in random and needless projects, I began to take on more and more of his neglected responsibilities, including mounting an investigation of this fusing of worlds that's taken place. That's where my man Asherby came in," Roosevelt said, patting the tall man on the shoulder. "Unfortunately, it seems our poking about stirred things up a bit, as the next thing I know, the city is under attack by these fairy folk. We held out as long as we could, but there were too many of them and we were no match for their bizarre weapons. I was able to gather the remaining troops and pull back to the White House."

"Why aren't you there now?" Maga asked.

"Because," Roosevelt scowled, "as soon as those cursed fey set up camp on Capitol Hill and started chanting in that strange, alien language, the President turned."

"Turned?" Manchester said with surprise.

"He became one of them," Roosevelt said. "And he started chanting with them... same blasted words his would-be assassin used. Some of the soldiers joined him, as though they were hypnotized or brainwashed. I was able to send the President's family and my own family to safety outside the city before I escaped and set up operations in the tunnels with what few soldiers I could recruit. Those of us who remain have been down here for weeks now, popping up every once in a while to harass the fey or send some of these dead men back to their graves."

"My question is," Manchester started, "how did your bullets kill the Baymaari?"

"*Baymaari?*" Roosevelt said with surprise. "Is that what they're called? We've been calling them *vampires*, for lack of a better term... like in the book by that Irish fellow... Stoker, I believe is his name. Anyway, that being our line of thinking, one of my more devout men took to carving the sign of the cross on the tips of his bullets. We noticed his shots finally put the heathens to rest, so we all began doing it."

"Yes. Of course," Manchester said. "The cross is a symbol of hope. The Baymaari wouldn't be able to tolerate it."

"Now, I have a few questions of my own, if you don't mind," Roosevelt said.

Maga nodded. "Go ahead, sir."

"These Baymaari are the dead come back to life, correct?"

"Sometimes," Manchester answered. "The soldiers you dispatched in the tunnels were clearly undead. But we suspect the Áes dána that have taken over Washington are mostly alive."

"So it's like some kind of demon possession?" Roosevelt asked.

"More like a sentient disease," Asherby broke in. "I've seen both live and dead Baymaari. The live ones move more quickly and seem to have intelligence. The dead ones are just empty shells acting on some rudimentary instinct."

"And then there are the *Culst Mardarri*," Manchester added. "You and Bugbear ran into one of those at the unseelie camp."

"Yes," Asherby said. "Duergar. He was undead, but clearly a thinking creature."

Roosevelt took another sip of coffee. "So essentially, we're up against an enemy that adapts to whatever the situation requires. If brute force is needed, they use the dead. If more subtlety and cunning is required, they'll possess the living. And if they need both, they'll instill one of the dead with a demonic intelligence."

"Yes," Manchester said. "We suspect the Culst Mardarri act as their generals, while the others are mere foot soldiers."

Roosevelt dumped the remainder of his coffee to the ground. "The doctor said William's heart was shredded by the assassin's bullet," he said with a tremble. "That there was no way he should have been able to survive." The Vice President grunted to his feet, wiping the coffee from his mustache with a handkerchief. "I suspect now that he didn't survive after all."

"You think President McKinley is dead?" Asherby gasped.

"It makes sense now," Roosevelt said. He strode over to a regional map tacked to the cavern wall. "Shortly after his 'recovery' the President began reassigning troops from the garrison here in Washington. Sending them to Arlington, Sharpsburg, even as far off as Gettysburg."

"Lots of war dead in those towns," Manchester mused.

"Indeed," Roosevelt nodded grimly. "I can only imagine if the Baymaari have infected those areas, our brave young men were sent to their dooms. And with them away from Washington, we were ill equipped to hold off the Áes dána assault."

"So the siege is as much due to sabotage from inside as an attack from outside," Maga concluded.

"Indeed," Roosevelt replied. "William even ordered workmen to rewire the telegraph and telephone lines. So when the assault did happen, our communication lines were down and we were unable to order in additional troops."

"So," Manchester started, "with an ever increasing hold on the Áes dána, and the United States capitol in its clutches, the Baymaari would face little resistance from the other races. The ogres are pacifist, the goblins are too disorganized, and the dwarves are preoccupied with mining."

"The battle isn't over yet, Martin," Maga interrupted. "A good portion of the Áes dána army is represented here, but they haven't all been turned. Plus, you forget about my sisters."

"Yes," Roosevelt nodded. "The dragon brides. We came across a few of them last week. Helped us in a skirmish against the Áes dána. Said they were looking for some chap named *Bugaloo*, I believe."

"Bugbear," Manchester laughed.

"That was it," Roosevelt said as he huffed on his glasses and polished them with his handkerchief. "Quite sorry to see them leave. An awesome and glorious thing to watch them in battle."

"Did they say which direction they were heading?" Maga asked, her voice heavy with concern.

"Just passing through on their way west," Roosevelt said. "I suggested they follow the railroad tracks for the most direct route."

"That would have taken them past Cron," Maga whispered to Manchester as she placed her hand on his chest.

"Like the Vice President said, they're born warriors," Manchester said, pulling Maga close and running his hands through her dark hair. "If they did run into Cron, she's the one whose life would be at risk."

Vice President Roosevelt placed his glasses back on his nose, gazing at his meager forces and placing a hand on the hilt of his Colt. "Well, my friends," he said in a vibrant and clear bell-like voice, "since this war started with sabotage from within, let us end it likewise."

"How so, Mister Vice President?" Asherby asked.

"We shall storm the White House," Roosevelt answered, slapping Asherby on the back. "And we shall give William the honor of a true death."

"You mean...?" Asherby stammered.

"Yes," Roosevelt hissed. "We shall assassinate the President of the United States... again."

CHAPTER 28
OVER THE RAINBOW

Few Baymaari guarded the parameter near the Bilröst barrier. Bugbear imagined the Culst Mardarri leaders felt (well, if they *felt* anything at all) there was little need to keep watch over such an insurmountable blockade. So, as Bugbear, Brenen, Threelgon, and Rígan flew the tylluans through the light, gray drizzle and over the barrier, they were met with meager resistance. Consequently, Bugbear insisted Threelgon use no force against them. They were, after all, innocent Áes dána, infected by an insidious and intelligent disease.

As they landed the tylluans just over the wall, a handful of the living Baymaari (what Bugbear had taken to calling *Jandaari*) rushed towards them. Bugbear was the first to dismount, and so took the initiative in confronting the guards.

"Watch and learn, Threelgon," Bugbear laughed as he rushed towards the Jandaari.

"Little maniac," Threelgon huffed as he tied off the tylluans to a nearby post.

Much quicker of reflex and wit than their dead brethren, the Jandaari charged Bugbear with swords drawn. The goblin noticed their blades were Áes dána *lonraigh*, a particularly devastating weapon drenched in alchemical flame... one touch, and the fire would bypass flesh and muscle, burning right to the marrow of the bone. Bugbear knew that moving this event would require delicate orchestration.

The goblin stopped, humming and waving his arms at the Jandaari. The Jandaari ceased their charge, looking about as Bugbear's hum seemed to surround them like a swarm of bees. Snarling with frustration, they swung their swords at the unseen nuisance. Bugbear's fingers danced with graceful precision, guiding the sound between and around the pack of possessed warriors, causing them to swing their blades in specific and calculated maneuvers. The blades cut and tore and rendered armor and tunics and belts. Finally, as Bugbear's humming stopped, the Jandaari warriors stood stark and exposed in their undergarments, the soft, misting rain drenching their shivering forms. Dark, gray clouds smoldered out of their trembling forms, the Baymaari infection driven from them in wailing defeat. The bewildered Áes dána dropped their swords and began frantically picking through their discarded armor and clothing.

"Would have been better off killing them," Threelgon snorted as he walked up behind Bugbear.

"Actually, we'll need their uniforms," Bugbear said. "You don't need to kill them. But it wouldn't hurt to make them think you will."

"With pleasure," Threelgon said, drawing his sword and advancing on the Áes dána.

"I thought it took hope to defeat the Baymaari," Rígan laughed as she watched Threelgon roust the mortified warriors.

"As the great and noble Twistroot once wrote: *'The road called Hope is traveled by a thousand humiliations.'*"

Threelgon frowned as he returned with an armful of armor and clothing, the vanquished Áes dána having fled towards a nearby stable. The unseelie prince threw a uniform at Brenen's feet. "Here," he snarled. "You can have the garments of the one who humiliated his trousers."

"Nonsense," Bugbear said, waving off Threelgon. "Brenen and I shall be sharing a uniform. So we'll take one that hasn't been soiled, thank you very much."

Threelgon snickered as he kicked away the dirty clothing and armor and handed Bugbear a clean set.

"Share?" Brenen said, his face puckered by doubt.

"Yes," Bugbear answered, handing the clothing up to him. "I'm too short to fit into a uniform of my own. But I've found through experience that I ride quite well on the backs of others. Simply pretend you're a hunchback."

"Yes. Another deformity to seal my unseelie fate," Brenen sighed as he began donning the uniform.

"Once we bluff our way past the Baymaari hordes," Bugbear started as he looked off in the distance towards Capitol Hill, "we should find an island of safety on the Capitol steps."

"Why is that?" Rígan asked, her face barely visible through an ill-fitting helmet.

"My dear queen," Bugbear said with a knowing smile, "haven't you wondered why the Baymaari are camped around the buildings of the National Mall, but dare not enter them?"

"I assumed they were starving out the civilian authorities inside," Rígan sighed as she tried to right the awkward, towering helmet.

"A logical conclusion," Bugbear nodded. "But the true answer lies in Non-Logic. You see, the stone used for the foundation of many of the buildings on Capitol Hill, including the Capitol Building, the Library of Congress, and the Supreme Court, were quarried at Wigginton Island."

"Wigginton Island?" Rígan said, holding the wobbling helmet in place with both hands. "I've heard of that."

"Yes," Bugbear laughed, the joy of knowledge skittering through his brain like a swarm of spiders. "Like Tamarack Mountain, Wigginton is a nexus point that simultaneously existed on both Annwfn and the human world. And it was at Wigginton those countless ages ago that Whittlegrip and Reginald fashioned the first

Noggle Stones."

"While they were at it, could they have fashioned a helmet that fits a normal person's head?" Rígan raged as she finally threw the awkward headgear to the ground. "Really, Brenen? This is what you were able to accomplish after I left the throne? Redesigning the army's helmets into these... these monstrosities?"

Brenen looked to the ground, nudging the discarded helmet with his foot. "I thought they would look imposing in battle. Like the dragons of old."

"Battle is not about appearances," Threelgon spat. "It's about tactics and strategy!"

"Excuse me," Bugbear grumbled as he stomped between the arguing unseelie. "Do not interrupt my vital exposition with your pointless digressions!" Bugbear struggled with the unwieldy helmet, dragging it back to Rígan. "Besides," the goblin sputtered, "as awkward as they are in battle, Brenen's helmets make for the perfect disguise as we navigate through the Baymaari camp. Now put it on!"

Rígan frowned at the little man, clearly upset by his lack of respect.

Bugbear glared back at her, clearly angered by her lack of discipline.

Rígan turned from the goblin's gaze, released a sharp breath, and bent down to take up the monstrous helmet.

Bugbear's face relaxed into a smile. "Excellent! Now I can continue my brilliant observations." The goblin paced back over to gaze at Capitol Hill, its monuments and buildings hazy on the horizon. "As I was saying, the very stone quarried at Wigginton to lay the foundations of those buildings, was the same stone used for the first Noggle Stones games. Thus, the Baymaari are repulsed by the special metaphysical significance that permeates these structures."

"Like salt to a leech," Brenen observed.

"Exactly!" Bugbear piped to Brenen with an upraised finger. "Brilliant analogy!" The goblin waddled up to the disgraced king and patted him on the back. "Of course you mustn't take any of the credit for yourself. It's entirely due to my influence."

"Shall we go now?" Rígan asked, exasperated as she shoved bits of discarded cloth between her head and her helmet to make the fit more secure.

"Of course," Bugbear said. The goblin motioned to Brenen with a deep flourish. "Your hunch is waiting, Brenen."

Brenen grumbled as he got down to one knee and bowed, allowing Bugbear access to his back. The goblin clambered on, settling up near the king's shoulders. Brenen covered his passenger with a cloak as he groaned into a stand.

"I suggest we behave as dead Baymaari," Bugbear said, peeking out from beneath the cloak. "Less likely to be questioned by the Jandaari or Culst Mardarri."

Threelgon and Rígan nodded and then shambled forward, arms hanging loose at their sides and mouths pulled into low moans.

"A good start," Bugbear said, his voice bubbling with encouragement. "But bend down more, and make those moans more... tortured."

The unseelie siblings did as instructed, shuffling down the streets, their voices the very personification of misery and torment.

"Well," Brenen clucked as he followed the faux zombies, "nice to see someone else the victim of your cruel sense of humor."

"About that," Bugbear sighed, shifting himself on Brenen's shoulders, "I have a confession, Brenen."

"Oh?"

Bugbear sat silent for a few moments, his tongue conspiring with his mind to summon just the right words. "Back at the army camp," he finally started, "the medics made a clerical error."

"About me?" Brenen asked, his voice trembling with panic. "Is the wound worse than I thought? Is it spreading?"

"There is no wound," Bugbear grunted. "One of the doctors mixed your chart up with another patient's. He saw a bit of raspberry tart smeared on your face and assumed it was blood from the wound."

"Then I... I'm not unseelie," Brenen stammered.

"No," Bugbear replied. "And you're still a king."

Brenen turned about, violently reaching at Bugbear with wild slaps and punches. "You lied to me!"

"I did not," Bugbear hissed, dodging about beneath the cloak as he clung precariously to Brenen's back. "I simply neglected to reveal the truth to you. Now, please stop yelling at your hump. You're going to draw attention."

Brenen's eyes went wide as he realized they were now walking in the midst of the Baymaari camp.

The warriors' clouded eyes regarded the hobbling spies with dull indifference, more intent in their ceaseless mumbling than rooting out spies and saboteurs.

"Why?" Brenen whimpered to Bugbear. "Why would you do something so cruel? You know how important appearance is to the Áes dána, especially royalty."

"Exactly," Bugbear whispered. "You needed to be shown that appearance and position are not nearly as important as duty and devotion. You needed to become the lowest of the low before you could be allowed to return to your throne."

"And what gives you the right to decide this?" Brenen spat.

"Because," Bugbear huffed, "I went through the same thing. I was enslaved by the Shadow Smith. The humiliation. The pain. The suffering. When I crawled out of that pit of shame, I emerged a better person... a better friend." Bugbear closed his eyes, trying to wash away the bitter memories. When he blinked his red-ringed eyes open again, conviction seized his voice. "So you see, I didn't take anything from you, Brenen. I gave you a great gift."

Brenen continued shambling after Threelgon and Rígan, watching as the sun glinted off an exposed part of the queen's silver arm. "And what do I do now?" the king sighed. "Return to my tiny kingdom and squabble with my rivals over the scraps of the old Empire?"

Bugbear offered a soft and reassuring smile as he patted Brenen on the back. "There are three reasons people exist, Brenen," he whispered. "Some are here to make things better. Some are here to make things worse. And some are here simply to be caught in the middle. But we all have a choice as to which we want to be, my friend. Choose your reason to exist, Brenen."

Brenen looked to the ground, his face empty and blank. A thin worm of guilt burrowed deep into Bugbear's conscience. A year ago, the Shadow Smith had deceived and humbled him, toppling him from his lofty birthright as Whittlegrip's heir, enslaving him as a lowly tea boy. And now Bugbear had done much the same to Brenen... tricking him away from his throne and herding him into life as an owl-keeper. And while the goblin's intentions were certainly more pure, the results could have been no less devastating for the Áes dána king. At least the Shadow Smith had been honest about who he was and his plans of conquest. Whereas Bugbear had essentially betrayed someone with whom he sought an alliance... someone whom he had even begun to consider a friend.

As to where the events Bugbear had moved would lead them now, the goblin had his doubts. And even though he had left the choice in Brenen's hands, should the plan crumble to failure and the Baymaari claim victory, the blame was Bugbear's and his alone.

CHAPTER 29
DEAD PRESIDENT

In the flickering lantern light Vice President Roosevelt ran his fingertips along the edges of the bricks in the wall before him. "Blasted Jefferson!" he spat. "Leave it to a Virginian to design a secret door that's so secret it can't be found!"

Manchester placed a hand on the Vice President's shoulder. "And leave it to a failed stage magician to find what's right in front of a New Yorker's nose," the king chuckled.

Roosevelt stepped back into the tunnel, his brows raised as he waved Manchester towards the wall. "By all means, lad."

Manchester lifted his finger and counted the bricks blocking the doorway. "17," he said as he pushed the 17th brick from the top and from the left. The brick moved in and the wall rotated, opening a gap.

"How did you know?" Roosevelt laughed, slapping Manchester on the back.

Manchester lurched forward and sputtered from the force of the Vice President's enthusiasm. "There were 17 states in the Union during Jefferson's presidency," Manchester explained as he regained his balance. "Plus, that brick had a dark oil stain from where people had been pressing it all these years."

"By Jiminy!" the Vice President erupted as he placed his arm about Manchester's shoulder. "I imagine a crackerjack like you would make a splendid sparing partner. Ever do any boxing, lad?"

"I can vouch for that," Pope stepped forward with a knowing smirk.

Maga discretely wedged her way in front of Roosevelt and Manchester. "Mister Vice President," she said in a hushed tone, "typically I'd be more indulgent in your amusement at my husband's expense. However, I believe caution is in order. We're about to enter the lion's den, to use a metaphor you might appreciate."

"Good point, my dear," Roosevelt said, lowering his voice and removing his arm from Manchester's shoulder. He unsheathed his Colt and stepped through the opening in the wall. "Follow me," he urged.

The others stepped through the crack in the wall, finding themselves in one of the opulent and well-decorated halls of the White House.

"Why isn't your house as nice as this, King Munchausen?" Riley asked as he padded past the great portraits and statues.

"Because I don't have 125 years of history to put on display, wisenheimer," Manchester answered with a chuckle.

"The Executive Offices are up ahead," Roosevelt said as he cautiously trod along the soft oriental carpet.

Asherby took a position just behind the Vice President, carrying a rifle he had borrowed from one of Pope's men.

Maga drew her sword, an uneasy edge to her silver eyes as she peered down the corridor.

Manchester fell in beside her, pulling out his pistols and trying to follow her fitful glances. "You sense something?" he asked softly.

"No," she whispered. "And that's what bothers me. From what Asherby said, this building should be swarming with soldiers, here to protect the President." Maga sighed and shrugged. "But I know the echoes of an empty house. We're alone here, Martin."

Manchester puckered his lips in thought. "Riley," he suddenly whispered.

The patchwork trotted up to the king. "Yes?"

"Do you smell anyone else here besides us?" Manchester asked.

Riley raised his muzzle to the air, his canine nose twitching and snorting. "No. Just us. And something dead."

"Something dead?" Maga said.

"Lots of something dead," Riley elaborated as he scowled and covered his snout. "And chemicals."

"Baymaari?" Manchester said to Maga.

"Well, we at least know McKinley is infected," the dragon bride replied. "Perhaps he did away with the soldiers?"

"Using his chemistry set?" Manchester grunted.

Asherby rushed back to them, his face smothered in a white sheet of alarm. "You need to hurry now!" he blurted, pulling Manchester by the shoulder.

"What is it?" Manchester asked as he, Maga, and Riley ran after the tall man.

"A big, *big* problem," Asherby answered.

The sound of gunfire punched their ears, and the smell of gunpowder bit their noses. One of Pope's men soared past the foursome, cracking plaster and jarring brick as he slammed into a wall. By the time they rounded the corner to the Executive Office, five more men had either fallen or were being hefted into the air by a grotesque mound of flesh and bone.

"What in the name of...?" Manchester exclaimed. His disbelieving eyes bulged as he beheld a huge and monstrous creature that seemed to be molded together by a deranged sculptor... bits and pieces from different body parts jammed and jabbed and slammed together. Arms and legs writhed and twined in a mass of intermingled torsos. Mouths screamed from chests and backs. Eyes winked and stared from feet and shoulders and bottoms. And at the top of the writhing mound one lone figure loomed, his head, shoulders and torso the only recognizably human composition in the creature's make-up. "President McKinley?" Manchester gasped.

Roosevelt, Pope, and the soldiers fired their weapons, but even the sacred bullets seemed to have no effect on the rumbling pile of fused corpses.

"Give up... Teddy!" McKinley's head mocked. "You can't defeat what's inside you... Teddy!"

"Don't call me Teddy!" Roosevelt thundered as he fired off another round into the mound of evil.

The bullets sank into the massive pile of flesh and bone, but the mouths that pocked its bloated surface merely laughed at the feeble assault. Huge, inhuman arms wrapped and combined with sinew and muscle from other body parts stretched out and grasped the beleaguered soldiers, smashing them into the walls, ceiling, and floor. Blood and brain painted the room, like a madman's wallpaper.

Gray ash billowed from pustules sprouting across the creature's skin. The cloud of infection fell over the crowd of freedom fighters, choking and suffocating close to a dozen of the men in the room. Those infected briefly fell to their knees as they struggled against the Baymaari microbes... but the potent plague overtook them, and they rose with blank faces and dull eyes to attack their former allies.

Now the ragtag rebels fought not only the grotesque hill of dead flesh, but a troop of fresh Jandaari, armed with guns. The bullets ricocheted through the small office, slicing through the air like lead lightning, striking down free and infected alike. Already cramped and enclosed, the allies began to falter. Some fell to gunfire, others fled the room. And the freshly slain rose again to join the Jandaari. Soon, only Manchester, Maga,
Riley, Asherby, Pope, and Roosevelt remained. And while their bullets dispatched the Jandaari and Baymaari dead, the great mound of undead flesh that spawned them withstood the attacks,

continuing to spew its gray poison into the air.

Manchester fired his twelve-shooters at the creature as he ran up beside the Vice President. "Mr. Roosevelt, we need to get out of here! The Baymaari have used Coranieid alchemy to merge the President with his guards! It's hopeless!"

"Nonsense!" the Vice President exclaimed. "There's always hope!" He fired another round, followed by a click. "Cover me while I reload, boy!"

Manchester grumbled, firing his guns at the lurching monstrosity as the Vice President reloaded his Colt. Then a wild and stray thought suddenly nested in the king's head. "Asherby!" he called back to the tall man.

"Yes?" Asherby replied as he fired his rifle at the beast.

"You still have that letter you wrote to Rígan?"

The tall man bit his lip and fired another shot. "Yeah."

"Read it to us!" Manchester shouted.

"What? I'm not going to do that!"

"Read it!" Manchester ordered again. "Hope is the only way to stop this thing! And a man with a civil servant's salary in love with a fairy queen is about as hopeful as you can get!"

"I... I'm not in love with her!" Asherby protested.

"Just read it!" Maga grumbled as she lunged forward with her blade.

Asherby breathed sharply as he looked to Riley. "If you ever fancy a girl, don't write it down," he muttered, removing the paper from his inside pocket. "Someone will just use it against you."

Riley nodded as he nocked an arrow and fired on the undulating mass of dead men.

Asherby sighed and cleared his throat. "My dearest Rígan," he mumbled.

"Louder!" Roosevelt said, his voice ringing over the gunfire.

"My dearest Rígan!" Asherby shouted. "I once told a friend that when I settled down with the right woman, our children would have ancestors whose stories stretched back to the dawn of time and across all four corners of the globe!"

McKinley sputtered and sneered. "Tell your parrot to keep quiet... Teddy!"

"Ha!" Roosevelt laughed as he fired his pistol. "Read on, Asherby!"

"They would be as American as the mountains, and rivers, and forests around them!" Asherby called out, his voice louder and clearer. "But in their veins would flow the promise of a better world!"

McKinley twisted and cracked his neck, his vertebrae popping like embers in a fire. "Teddy... why don't you join us?" The President's lifeless flesh contorted and oozed like melted wax, as something resembling a smile crossed his blood-flecked lips.

"Damn this abomination!" Roosevelt cursed.

"Pay no attention, Mister Vice President!" Manchester said. "It's using words to inspire despair, just was we are using words to inspire hope." The magician-king turned to Asherby. "Read louder, man!"

"And even though I voiced this dream," Asherby continued, "I had in my heart known it to be foolish and beyond the grasp of such a simple man! Until I saw your radiant form! Until I felt your healing hands! Until I heard your songbird voice!"

"*Songbird voice?*" Riley snickered.

"This is ridiculous, Manchester," Asherby scowled as he lowered the crumpled letter. "We need to fall back, gather more troops, and take the city by force."

"I agree," Pope said, leveling his rifle at the advancing puppet-soldiers. "Readin' poetry to the blasted critters ain't gonna hurt them as much as it tortures us."

Manchester snarled as he fired his twelve-shooters into the mound of writhing flesh. "Listen, you idiots! Our war with the Baymaari will not be won with weapons. This is a conflict if ideals. A battle that can only be won with words!" Manchester paused to kick a crawling orphaned hand away from his foot. "So you read that wretched letter, Asherby! You speak every cliché-crusted crumb! You say every sugar-saturated syllable! You speak every maudlin-matted mouthful until your throat is raw with romance and your tongue swollen with sentiment!"

Asherby shook his head and frowned as he lifted the crumpled paper to read once more. "Whether or not I'm worthy of you," he continued, "I want you to know that I am grateful simply to have met you!"

As Asherby read the letter, the Baymaari homed in on him, like sharks drawn to a drop of blood. Pope and Riley stood before the secret service agent, firing rifle and bow to keep the undead hordes at bay. Pope seemed to have a particularly difficult time shooting at some of his own soldiers, but he gritted his teeth and did his duty all the same.

"Shoot to wound the ones that are still alive," Pope said, leaning towards the patchwork. "We might be able to kill the disease without killing the victims."

Riley nodded in understanding as he touched his paw to the medallion Pfeil had given him, infusing his arrows with that whisper of sacred hope needed to destroy the Baymaari infection.

"I don't pretend to understand how I could have become so smitten so quickly," Asherby read. "Perhaps you have placed me under a spell. If so, then I gladly accept this enchantment. Let witchcraft take my wits. For I would gladly be your dumb and dutiful dupe before returning to the empty life I led before."

The mound of dead flesh shuddered and trembled. "Oh, Teddy!" McKinley moaned. Manchester, Roosevelt, Pope, and the rest continued to fire their guns, the creature now howling and undulating in pain at each bullet that struck its fleshy bulk. Between Asherby's saccharine sentiments and the sanctified ammunition, the Baymaari abomination weakened and withered.

"Beneath the warmth of your crystal blue gaze," Asherby resumed, "my dying dream was rekindled! And even if I never lay eyes upon your beauty again, just having been in your glorious presence, I now truly believe in the promise of a better world!"

As the room fogged with the thick stench of gun powder and the echo of Asherby's words reverberated off the blood-caked walls, the heap of corpses crumbled, falling into moist pieces and parts on the smooth marble floors.

"Thank goodness," Riley heaved a sigh as he lowered his bow. "Any more of that and we would have fallen apart as well."

"Yeah!" Asherby blurted defensively as he shoved the letter back into his pocket. "You're welcome!"

The Vice President quietly stepped through the pile of dead parts, standing over the writhing form of McKinley. The Baymaari infected President floundered in the midst of the putrid pile, reaching out with hands curled and gnarled by rigor mortis.

"Theodore..." the undead creature hissed.

Roosevelt set his jaw firmly, and behind his spectacles his eyes turned hard and wet. "I don't know if I can do it," he whispered.

Maga sheathed her sword and stepped up beside him. "Mr. Vice President, he's already dead. He's been dead for a very long time."

"But he's my President," Roosevelt said softly. "He's my friend."

"Then put your friend to rest," Manchester said, placing a hand upon his shoulder.

Roosevelt took a deep breath and nodded. "Goodbye, William. And God speed."

The Colt .38 echoed through the White House, putting an end to the Baymaari invasion of the White House, and sending the 25th President of the United States on to the next world.

Maga and Manchester pulled the stunned Roosevelt away from the pile of corpses as the Baymaari cloud rose from the carnage and flowed out the open window with a bone-chilling howl.

Asherby, Pope, and Riley tended to the wounded soldiers as the room settled into an eerie and uneasy silence. Maga poked at the dead body parts with the tip of her blade. "Not your typical Baymaari foot soldiers," she noted.

"I suspect it was a kind of *queen*," Manchester said. "The Baymaari most likely used Cron's alchemy to mix the corpses together, creating an undead incubator for the infection. If we hadn't killed it, I imagine it would have started pumping Baymaari bacteria into the air, causing a mass epidemic all across the eastern United States."

Roosevelt walked to the window, watching after the gray mass of infection as it dissolved in the sky. He shook his head as he polished his glasses with a handkerchief. "I wanted to be President," he said, "but I did not want to become President this way."

Manchester strolled up behind the new President, placing a hand upon his shoulder and peering across the lawn towards Capitol Hill. "You'll be an excellent Commander-in-Chief, sir," the king said. "I just hope Bugbear can set the rest of your capital free."

CHAPTER 30
DANU'S CHILDREN

Shambling in silence for what seemed hours through the mumbling hordes, the party of infiltrators finally reached the steps of the Capitol Building. Bugbear jumped from Brenen's back and began scurrying up the steps.

"Quickly!" the goblin called to his companions. "We need to get to higher ground."

The goblin's three allies followed, shedding their disguises. Brenen tugged and tore at his bandages, unwinding them with frustration and impatience.

Rígan stayed back, walking with him up the steps. "He told you?"

"Yes," Brenen grumbled as he discarded the bandages and placed trembling fingertips to his smooth and unblemished face. "You were in on it?"

Rígan nodded. "I had my doubts, but I'd always been taught it's best not to cross a goblin with secrets."

"And Bugbear seems to have more secrets than most," Brenen snorted.

"I was surprised you didn't figure it out for yourself, considering there wasn't any physical pain," Rígan noted.

"Having never been wounded before, I didn't know what to expect."

Rígan rubbed her flesh and blood hand along her silver arm. "I can assure you," she shuddered, "there is pain."

"I wanted your throne so badly," Brenen said with a deep breath as they continued up the massive steps. "But not like that. I had nothing to do with the *fealltóir cabal* that planned your downfall."

"I know," Rígan smiled, placing the back of her silver hand gently on his cheek.

Brenen inhaled as he fought back the tears burning at the edges of his eyes. He softly kissed the back of her hand. "We were so close when we were children."

"I was always the Noggle Lord," Rígan laughed as she lowered her hand and took a hold of his.

"I won a few games," Brenen smirked. His face then faded to stone as he turned to his cousin with deep and sorrowful eyes. "But you were always the leader. Always the smartest and the best." The tears fell free now, rolling down his pristine ivory cheeks. "Right now I hate that goblin more than any creature on earth. And yet, he was right. He did give me a great gift. For he reunited us. And I remember now how deeply I care for you... how that radiant crown of red hair glows like the sun, and those wise blue eyes sparkle like dew. How every word you utter seems to be just right and so perfect and always needed."

"Brenen," Rígan whispered as she squeezed his hand tighter.

"Go, Rígan," Brenen said, releasing her hand and pointing off to Bugbear and Threelgon who stood at the top of the steps. "The goblin awaits."

Rígan hesitantly parted from Brenen, hiking up the hem of her skirt as she ascended the stone steps. Brenen lingered behind, his feet slow and uncertain.

"Your cruelty hasn't gone unnoticed, goblin," Rígan huffed as she joined Bugbear and Threelgon.

"You can't pile any more guilt on my heart than I've already stacked there myself," Bugbear replied. "So, save some for yourself. After all, I wasn't the one who made Brenen an owl-keeper."

Rígan looked to Bugbear with knitted brow. "Tell me your plan then," she muttered. "Perhaps we can both do penance by ending this."

Bugbear grumbled and reached into his coat pocket, shortly producing a fist-sized metal orb with tiny holes pocking the surface. "I nicked this from the Dabblers," he said, handing the object to Rígan. "I believe it was to be the voice box for their mechanical lady. I've taken the liberty of making a few adjustments, which should make it an effective voice amplifier."

"And what exactly am I supposed to say?" Rígan asked as she rolled the strange device over in her silver hand.

"I will feed you the lines," Bugbear said. "You shall repeat them in Dragon Speak."

"They've already noticed us," Threelgon reported as he nudged Bugbear and Rígan and pointed down the steps at the great mass of Baymaari infected Áes dána sprawled across the mall. The blank-faced warriors stirred, rising and shambling towards the steps, yet lingering just beyond, repulsed by the Non-Logical energy permeating the foundations of Capitol Hill.

"Then we have a ready audience," Bugbear said, cocking his head to Rígan. "Time to reclaim your Empire."

Bugbear and Threelgon retreated behind Rígan as she gazed out towards the vast army. She raised her silver arm in the sky, the sunlight dancing along its edges, giving it an eerie, otherworldly sparkle. With her other hand she brought the voice box to her mouth. She looked back to Bugbear and nodded.

"After many long years your queen has returned, whole and ready to reclaim the throne," Bugbear whispered to Rígan,

"Brud buhu tuleel surn durmap Markla har wurpur pula aoz taior raf wurpulc shulmadeen," Rígan intoned through the amplifier, her voice taking on an weird and everywhere sound.

"Our great Empire shall likewise be made whole... reborn as a bright new beacon in this strange new world."

"Mapdur aalzem Qumar kayn geebhi buh ultak pula... puldur hon dob jusur naya rosheer anduv aik ajoz naya jauzub."

"Join me in this great endeavor," Bugbear continued whispering to Rígan. "Join me as the Empire of our ancestors rises once more!"

"Juldna mulhay anduv aik alzuhm jul-uh-judeed," Rígan repeated through the voice box. *"Juldna mulhay hon Qumar mapdur hanuuruu aanaa-o-uunuu ultna ak-du-aur."*

The dumb warriors continued to mill about the steps, eying Rígan with dumb hatred and mumbling their mindless mantra: *"Durm taln nawneev larnawl kir har anduv durm."*

"Why isn't it working?" Bugbear wondered aloud. "Seeing their legendary queen restored to her glory should have them practically overflowing with hope."

"It's because you're only giving them words," Brenen broke in as he shuffled up the steps. "Words alone can't bring hope. There has to be meaning and emotion behind them. Trust me. When the Empire was crumbling around me, I gave speeches until my face was as purple as an ogre's. And the only time I ever reached anyone was when the words I spoke came from my own tongue and my own heart."

Bugbear looked to Brenen with a raised brow. "Then we could use that tongue and heart now, Brenen."

Brenen smiled as he gently grasped Rígan's hand. "Translate for me, my queen?"

Rígan nodded, her face filled with joy and relief.

Brenen stepped forward, his eyes set upon the horizon. He took a deep breath and released his shame. "I was a poor king," he said with a clear yet quavering voice. Rígan translated his words through the voice box. "My bottom sat easily on the throne, while the crown rested heavily on my brow. And it was my lack of vision, my inattention to policy, that led to the downfall of our great Empire. I was less your king and more your fool."

The Baymaari stirred, shambling up the steps, ignoring their aversion to the building's sacred stone foundation. *"Durm taln nawneev larnawl kir har anduv durm."*

"Well, that seemed to hit a chord," Bugbear said with surprise.

"I... I've made it worse," Brenen stammered.

"No, no, no," Bugbear laughed. "They wouldn't even be able to set foot on the steps if the Baymaari hold was complete. You've weakened them. Keep going!" The goblin laughed and excitedly motioned for Brenen to continue.

Brenen glared at the advancing warriors. And then suddenly, he turned his back and dropped to one knee. He took Rígan's silver hand in his and bowed his head before her. "I, Brenen, once High King of the Empire, now Sovereign of but a splinter of its former glory, pledge with what little honor I have left to support and serve the true Queen as she restores our great name and reputation, rebuilds our grand traditions, and renews our faith in a better tomorrow."

Taken aback by Brenen's display of submission, Rígan hesitated before translating the words into Dragon.

"Never should she have been denied her place in history as our greatest monarch," Brenen continued. "And never should we forget this day as she resumes that glorious destiny. For under her rule we all prosper, we all ascend to greater things, we all triumph over the enemies of hope."

Rígan repeated the words in Dragon, her voice trembling with emotion and her eyes brimming with tears.

The Baymaari chant ceased as the vast sea of warriors watched the unfolding drama on the Capitol steps.

Brenen raised his head to Rígan, his face awash in shame and regret. "I only hope," he stammered between his repentant sobs, "that she can forgive me and allow me to be her humble servant in the glorious struggle that lies ahead."

Rígan nodded as she bit her lip and let the tears flow freely. She knelt down and embraced Brenen, holding him tightly, burying her face into his shoulder.

Threelgon nudged Bugbear, drawing his attention to the multitudes below. The soldiers trembled and spasmed, the color and life returning to their faces, even as the gray ash billowed from their mouths. Soon the sky was a dark shroud of Baymaari infection, moaning and undulating... a dying nightmare.

Bugbear quickly took up the amplifier. "The Áes dána Empire is off your menu," he yelled to the gray expanse. *"Áes dána Qumar har des durmap zorhak."*

The Baymaari mass rumbled and screamed, sparking and boiling like a pregnant storm cloud.

"The High Queen reclaims the throne, and with her she brings peace!" Bugbear bellowed, almost shredding his vocal chords. *"Bulaar Markla wurpulc shulmadeen, aoz jolna zul zal lanu almur!"*

The edges of the collective began to fray, fizzle, and fade. The middle slowly collapsed and scattered, tiny particles gasping and crying out as the life burst from their centers.

"Go now, and leave these great nations to build great things on the ruins of your failure!" Bugbear commanded. *"Joa ahee, aoz charhnu aikee alzuhm wazul raf ultaka alzhum trumak andvu tobhur durmap noo-keenu!"*

The Baymaari shuddered a final, desperate death rattle, falling in on themselves and imploding like a sink full of dirty water spinning down the drain.

As the sunlight returned, the Áes dána warriors mumbled among themselves, trying to determine where they were and what had happened.

"Queen Rígan is whole again!" Bugbear called out to them through the voice box. "She shall ascend to the throne once more and reign as High Queen over the empire!" Bugbear waddled over to Rígan and Brenen. He gently raised Rígan's silver arm, taking Brenen's up with it as the queen firmly grasped his hand. "King Brenen is the first of the Draíocht Ridire to recognize her claim! Who shall stand with them as they rebuild the foundations of the Old Empire?"

A few enthusiastic shouts erupted through the crowd.

"Who shall forsake the folly of war for the certainty of peace?"

More voices joined the others in a chorus of optimism.

"All hail Queen Rígan!" Bugbear shouted. "All hail King Brenen! Danu bless the Empire!"

The entire mass of liberated soldiers repeated Bugbear's words, chanting them over and over in an ever-growing wave of joy and relief and hope.

"Good choice, Brenen," Bugbear whispered as he patted the redeemed monarch on the shoulder. "Much more satisfying than being caught in the middle, eh?"

Brenen nodded and smiled. "And easier than cleaning up tylluan droppings."

CHAPTER 31
THE PRESIDENT'S MOON SPEECH

The next few days the hands of many races, cultures, and nations joined together to rebuild the American capital. The Áes dána dissolved the Bilröst barrier. The American soldiers returned their deceased comrades to their graves. And Kings, Queens, and goblins sat in council with the President of the United States, negotiating treaties and alliances that would secure peace across a tumultuous land.

Brenen and a majority of the other Áes dána Kings and Queens (flown in for the meetings on tylluan-back) acknowledged Rígan's claim to rule as High Queen over the Áes dána empire. Her first act was to fold the Unseelie Court back into proper Áes dána society, granting them full rights and privileges as citizens of the Empire. Rather than favor a single royal house by selecting one of the current Áes dána Kingdoms as her capital, Rígan chose to rule the Empire from Willow Prairie, at the invitation of King Martin and Queen Maga.

The new President and new High Queen signed a formal treaty calling for an immediate cessation of all hostilities between the United States of America and the Áes dána Empire. Known as the *Bilröst Treaty*, the document also outlined a series of vigorous trade partnerships, as well as the sharing of technology, and cultural exchanges.

Furthermore, it was agreed that the United States would continue to hold sovereignty over her territories. All people (human and otherwise) living within those borders would be subject to American laws and policies. Empires, kingdoms, and principalities existing inside the United States would retain limited autonomy and, much like states, would send elected representatives to serve in the

Congress. Citizens of these communities would also be granted full American citizenship.

While President Roosevelt expressed his discomfort with having so many monarchies existing within United States territory, he acknowledged the importance of initiating a painless and tolerable transition to American rule. He charged King Martin and Queen Maga to be America's ambassadors to the fey nations, and gave them full authority to act on the United States government's behalf in any and all interactions with non-human regimes. In return, Willow Prairie would garrison a company of United States soldiers led by a newly promoted Captain Pope. Additionally, Asherby would act as the Roosevelt Administration's special liaison and serve in the newly created position of Secretary of Otherworldly Affairs... a position which Asherby quickly accepted when he learned his new office would be based in Willow Prairie.

All-in-all, the negotiations proved particularly satisfactory, if not completely ideal, to all involved. A general mood of goodwill and hope permeated the meetings from start to finish, and the overall consensus was that great friendships had been made and sturdy alliances had been forged.

"Excellent!" Bugbear piped as the final papers were signed, the last hands were shaken, and the remaining backs were patted. "Now, you should prepare a *crackerjack* speech, Mister President!" the goblin said to Roosevelt. "An entire nation will be listening!"

"Well, Washington will at least," Roosevelt said with a laugh. "Afraid the telegraph and telephone lines are still down, little man. The rest of the country will have to wait for the newspaper transcripts."

"Nonsense!" Bugbear said as he ran for the conference room door. "I have something in mind that will give you better coverage than telegraph, telephone, or television!" And with that, the goblin darted out the door, a deranged giggle trailing behind.

"What's *television*?" Roosevelt asked, leaning to Manchester.

"Probably something that hasn't been invented yet," Manchester shrugged. "Bugbear tends to be very forward thinking."

"By Jiminy!" Roosevelt laughed. "I could use a little pistol like him on my staff. Care to part with him, Martin?"

"Sorry, Mister President," Manchester smiled. "He's irreplaceable."

As evening gently rode in, various dignitaries and citizens gathered around the reflecting pool, where President Roosevelt was scheduled to give his speech at the base of the Washington Monument. Bugbear hurriedly directed Bixby and Cobblestone in some drastic redesigns and modifications on the remains of their mechanical lady.

"Poor ol' Matilda," Cobblestone sobbed. "She ain't never gonna see the light o' day at this rate."

"Oh, but she shall see the light of history, my friend," Bugbear said with a smile. "Once we've adjusted the receptive lenses in her eyes, and amplified the projection through the wires leading to the search reflectors I have set up, we shall initiate one of the most profound technological advances of the past 200 years!"

"Can we still call it Matilda?" Bixby asked as he took a pair of pliers to one of the wire connections.

"Certainly!" Bugbear laughed. "I can't think of a better name for such a beautiful device!"

The goblin left the Dabblers to their engineering duties as he scurried about fifty paces across to the other side of the stage. There a twelve foot high by eight foot wide mass of Bilröst crystal stood, its rainbow aura reaching up into the heavens. Bugbear had insisted the Áes dána leave at least a small fraction of the barrier for him to utilize in his experimental apparatus. The goblin checked the clamps and wires attached to the crystal, making certain the connection was secure. Confident that all was in place, Bugbear scampered up onto the stage where President Roosevelt, Manchester, Maga, and Rígan waited.

"Well, my fine young goblin," Roosevelt grunted, "is this *wonder-of-the-ages* going to be ready in this age I wonder?"

"But of course!" Bugbear chuckled. "A moment of patience, Mister President. We need to wait until the entire nation is under nightfall." Bugbear flipped open his pocket watch and observed the time. He raised a finger towards the Dabblers, who positioned the robotic head so that the eyes fell directly upon the President. The goblin pointed to them as his clock reached 11:05 p.m.

As the Dabblers pulled a lever on a small fuse box on the table beside them, Matilda's lenses lit up and bathed the President in a mild, gentle light. Various reflectors surrounding the stage collected the light, and with a steady, sturdy hum the electric wires carried the data to the Bilröst crystal. The crystal sparked with electrical agitation, causing some bystanders to retreat to a less "exciting" vantage point. The rainbow aura, undulating and wavering into the night sky above the crystal, narrowed and focused into a sharp beam. And that beam spiraled through the troposphere, punched through the stratosphere, sped through the mesosphere, thermosphere, exosphere... and finally through the inky, empty void of space, where it hit the surface of the full moon and exploded into a thousand pinpoints of color and light. The crowd gasped in amazement as the expanding light shimmered and settled over the entirety of the moon's surface, like a projection on a massive motion picture screen. Slowly the light focused and formed into a familiar visage... President Theodore Roosevelt.

"Congratulations, Mister President," Bugbear said with a bow. "You're the first man on the moon."

"How is this possible?" Roosevelt gasped as he gazed up in amazement at his own face on the moon.

"There are four basic precepts of Non-Logical Thought, which can never be repeated enough," Bugbear replied. *"Number one: Reality is Thought. Number two: Logic restricts Thought and thus restricts Reality. Number three: Abandon Logic, abandon restriction. And number four: Unrestricted Thought equals unrestricted Reality!"*

Roosevelt did not seem to hear the goblin, still baffled and mesmerized by the miracle of his own face looking down on him from the moon.

Bugbear smiled and handed the President Matilda's voice box, which was also connected to the crystal through wires. "Your country awaits, Mister President."

Roosevelt shook himself from his stupor and received the makeshift microphone. He cleared his throat and held the device near his mouth.

"The past year has seen a great many changes to our world," Roosevelt said, as his words echoed not only across Washington, but across the stratosphere and over the entire expanse of the American continent. "We have found ourselves inundated with new neighbors, new challenges, and new responsibilities. And in the chaotic storm that resulted, we have lost a man who was not only our President, but our friend." Roosevelt paused, taking a deep breath as though letting the immensity of the moment settle into his brain. "Yet as we mourn that loss, we celebrate what we have gained. New friends. New allies. New Americans. For the American way of life shall not only be preserved, it shall be enriched by an influx of new cultures and communities. While others may be content to trifle in war, we shall be committed to prosper in peace." The President looked over to Rígan, his face split into his famous and infectious grin as he took her silver hand in his.

"In history," he continued, "the difference between those who are remembered and those who are forgotten lies not in their ideologies, but in whether or not they supported those ideologies with real action. And in the days, weeks, and years to come you shall see action across this great nation of ours... great works performed by great people... vibrant advances in commerce and industry that shall be the envy of the world and the wonder of the ages." Roosevelt motioned to Rígan, Manchester, Maga, and Bugbear. "As your President, I have secured alliances and recruited great men and women... and, uhm, goblins... to serve this great vision of a United States more united than ever. Together we shall work for the promise of not only a better America, but a better world."

Rígan looked off stage and winked to Asherby. The tall man smiled and shyly removed his top hat as he offered her a slight bow.

"Go now, my friends," Roosevelt continued. "Go into tomorrow with strength, courage, and hope. For we are all God's children. We are all stewards of this vast and blessed land. And we are all... Americans."

The crowds lining the reflecting pool erupted in a hail of cheers and applause as Roosevelt concluded his speech. Bugbear tugged at Rígan's gown in an attempt to get her attention. The Queen smiled down at him.

"You can applaud now," Bugbear nodded.

Rígan looked down at her hands. They trembled slightly as the notion of what Bugbear said seemed to grip her. She slowly brought the hands together, then began to clap. She clapped louder, and louder, until she raised her hands above her head and cheered with the rest of the celebrants.

"Together we shall work for the promise of not only a better America, but a better world."

And all across America, likewise, multitudes of humans, Áes dána, dwarves, goblins, and ogres, all weary of war and doubt, raised their voices in joyous victory. And yet with that joy came also the realization that as much as he had given them hope, the President had also laid a challenge before them. But it was a challenge ripe with rewards for those bold enough to accept it... it was a challenge that for generations humans had called *"The American Dream."*

And so, on this night, the night President Roosevelt spoke from the moon, the Baymaari were dealt a devastating blow.

CHAPTER 32
HOMECOMING

Days later, the weary and victorious travelers returned to Willow Prairie. Bugbear, Tudmire, Pope, and the Dabblers journeyed by train, while Rígan, Threelgon, and Brenen traveled by tylluan. Asherby stayed behind in Washington a few extra days to settle his affairs before moving to Willow Prairie.

Maga had insisted that she, Manchester, and Riley return on horseback. It would take them roughly a week longer to return than the others, but those days would be spent wisely, as time with family always was.

Immediately after stepping off the train, Tudmire set about preparing the celebration for Riley's adoption. The seneschal had seldom taken so vigorously and enthusiastically to a task before. He made it his priority day and night until the royal family's return. Bugbear guessed the plump goblin had lost close to three stone, so intent he was in his duties that he skipped at least five of his 12 daily meals.

This left Bugbear to handle other tasks in the kingdom, such as assisting Pope in establishing the new garrison, and helping Rígan to choose her new accommodations.

"Where exactly will Howard's new office be located?" the queen asked Bugbear as they walked the streets of downtown Willow Prairie.

"Howard?" Bugbear said, his brow knitted with confusion.

"Mister Asherby," Rígan elaborated.

"Oh!" Bugbear chuckled. "Well, since we no longer have a Magistrate here in Willow Prairie, we thought we'd set him up over there." Bugbear motioned to a large, three-story brick manor house surrounded by a wrought iron fence. "It's actually probably much larger than what he needs," Bugbear continued with a raised eyebrow. "I was thinking we could convert the carriage house into his office and residence, and perhaps use the main house for another purpose."

"Do you suppose...?" Rígan started.

"Yes," Bugbear smiled. "It would make for an excellent royal embassy. And being in such close proximity to the office of the United States Secretary of Otherworldly Affairs would be convenient when you required... meetings, and such."

Rígan lowered her eyes and blushed lightly as she stepped across the street to examine the manor house more closely.

The goblin grunted with amusement to himself. "Better tell Tudmire to keep the good silver handy after the adoption ceremony. There will be an engagement party shortly following, I suspect."

Between his diplomatic duties, Bugbear also consulted with Bixby and Cobblestone on a secret project to be constructed on the front lawn of the newly rebuilt library. He implored the Dabblers to complete the undertaking before Manchester, Maga, and Riley returned. And so it was that Pope and his soldiers set up a tent for the Dabblers near the library from which much cursing and shouting could be heard as the inventors set about their secret task.

It was not too long before Asherby arrived in town on the train from Washington. With him was a modest staff of a file clerk and an army corporal. In addition, the newly appointed Secretary of Otherworldly Affairs (or S.O.A., as he preferred) brought the President's regrets that he could not attend the ceremony. Apparently the British Prime Minister made contact with the White House shortly after the telegraph lines were repaired. Having heard of America's successful treaties, the Prime Minister was hoping for some assistance in resolving Britain's own disputes with the

Tylwyth Teg, distant cousins of the Áes dána. Roosevelt felt the request an excellent opportunity to test the sea legs of his *Great White Fleet*, a Navy battle fleet he began secretly building when McKinley fell under Baymaari influence. He planned to lead the fleet himself, hoping to stretch his diplomatic muscles and demonstrate America's resolve to promote peace through unity.

"Ah," Bugbear said, upon hearing the news. "This Roosevelt is indeed as much a man of action as words. We're lucky to have such leadership."

"He sent this along with his apologies," Asherby said as he received a large, octagonal ceramic dish from his clerk. "Apparently it's from the Neolithic era. William Henry Harrison brought it to Washington from Indiana when he was elected President. Mister Roosevelt found it fitting it should return to Indiana."

"I'm certain the king and queen will appreciate the sentiment as well," Bugbear nodded.

As if the goblin's words were the last few crumbs on the bread trail home, Manchester, Maga, and Riley rode into the town square. The shouts of welcome trickled in slowly at first, as the news seeped and simmered through the town. But soon, all of Willow Prairie seemed to squeeze into the square, thronging about Manchester's and Maga's nektoshas and shouting out in joy and celebration.

"Welcome home!" Bugbear exclaimed as he nudged and budged his way through the merry mob. "I suggest you make haste in getting ready for the ceremony."

"But we just got here," Manchester protested.

"Understood," Bugbear replied. "But if we put this off any longer, poor old Tudmire will have wasted away to nothing but frayed nerves!"

As Pope's men led the nektoshas to the stables, Manchester,

Maga, Bugbear, and Riley made way to the old boarding house. There they found Tudmire barking orders to the staff and trying desperately to keep his saggy trousers from falling to the ground.

"Well, I hope you aren't going to attend the ceremony with your pants around your ankles," Manchester laughed as he entered the foyer.

"Ha ha!" Tudmire blurted as he spun about to see the royal family. "Just in time!" The jittery goblin waved a finger to one of the maids. "Abigail! Quickly! Go upstairs and draw a bath for the queen!" He then turned to one of the pages, waving his hands frantically. "Gerald! Go to the tailors and fetch King Martin's and Master Riley's suits!" Tudmire then turned about to the king, queen, and Riley as he caught his britches and pulled them up. "Well? Don't stand there! Hop to it! Ceremonies don't just sprout up spontaneously, you know!"

"You didn't need to go to all of this trouble, Tudmire," Maga said as she bent down and placed a hand aside his cheek.

"Of course I did," Tudmire said as he looked up to her with full, brimming eyes. "You're like family." And with a snuffle of his nose and shrug of his shoulders the goblin turned about to waddle towards the kitchen. "Oh, by the way!" he called back. "I found my pepper finally. But don't worry. I've taken a shine to turmeric of late."

Maga smiled after the goblin and then leaned in to give Manchester a quick peck. "Well, I'd better get to my bath then," she said. "I'll see you at the ceremony."

"Indeed you shall," Manchester said as he watched his wife go up the stairs.

Several hours later Manchester smoothed some hair cream into the fur atop Riley's head and struggled at it with a comb. "Stop fidgeting, Riley," the king grunted as he fought with the tangles.

"But it hurts, Pappy," Riley whined.

"I have a solution," Bugbear said as he sat up from his relaxed position on the nearby sofa. He pulled a feathered cap from his coat pocket. "Áes dána merchants are selling these outside. Seem to be quite the fashion."

Riley trotted up to Bugbear with his tail wagging. "It's just like Pfeil's," he said as he took it and placed it on his head.

Manchester walked over and knelt in front of Riley, adjusting the hat so it sat properly on the patchwork's head. "Matches the suit too," he observed.

Riley winced as he tugged at the uncomfortable bow tie. "Does being adopted mean I'll have to wear this terrible suit all the time?"

"Only when your mother tells you," Manchester replied as he tugged the tie back into place. "Now, go outside and wait in front of the library. Captain Pope will be waiting, and he told me he has another peppermint for you if you're good."

Riley lunged into Manchester with a strong and sturdy hug. "Thank you, Pappy."

Manchester returned the hug and smiled. "Thank you, son."

Then, after a quick lick to Manchester's face, the patchwork prince pranced out the door and into the festive streets outside.

"You do realize he just said *I* for the first time since he was turned into a patchwork?" Bugbear noted with interest as the boy left. "He's developed a sense of identity now. He's your son, a Prince of Willow Prairie."

"And you're his uncle," Manchester smirked as he looked himself over in the mirror.

"Good heavens!" Bugbear blurted. "I am! I suppose I'll be

expected to spoil him with candy and toys now."

"I'd prefer you discipline him with books and tutoring," Manchester sighed. "We've had a devil of a time keeping him in school."

"Well, I'll do my best to get him on the right track, Manchester," Bugbear said. "Perhaps he can join me in breaking in that new library. Still a few stray mysteries left over from our recent adventures."

"Oh?" Manchester said with interest as he turned about.

"Yes," Bugbear said as he held up the mysterious red book with the handwritten notes. "I have yet to determine when, how, and why I wrote all of these notes to myself."

"And we have to find out what happened to Maga's sisters," Manchester added.

"Not to mention the difficulties presented by the return of Duergar and Cron," Bugbear said. "Fortunately, we have plenty of new allies to assist us."

"As far as I'm concerned, it's a relief just to have you back," Manchester smiled.

Bugbear stroked his chin and exhaled. "Yes," he mused. "I have been gone a while."

"Well, you were doing important work," Manchester said.

"Perhaps." Bugbear said as he stood up from the sofa. "But I shan't wander far again, your Majesty."

"I believe I'll hold you to that promise, old friend," Manchester said as he walked up to the goblin and held out his hand.

Bugbear took the king's hand with both of his hands and gave it a solid shake. "So be it," he said. "The Royal Advisor is here to stay."

"Well, you best not be staying too long!" Tudmire snorted as he strolled through the open door. "Maga is waiting in front of the library right now! So unless you want to be tied to the skyrockets we're launching later tonight, I suggest you get moving!"

Bugbear nudged Manchester and laughed as he scurried out the door. Manchester chuckled and followed.

"Why is everybody laughing all the time?" Tudmire asked as he fell in behind them. "Celebrating is serious business!"

Moments later Manchester, Bugbear, and Tudmire joined Maga and Riley in front of the library. Pope and his men had removed the tent, and Bixby and Cobblestone stood nervously in front of a large, tall object covered by a tarp. A table was set up on the library lawn, where Tudmire had laid out the official adoption papers. The crowd of humans, Áes dána, ogres, and dwarves swarmed about the street in front. Rígan, Asherby, Threelgon, Brenen, Pope, and the ogre brothers were given seats of honor near the front.

Manchester stood beside Maga, looking into her silver eyes as he took her hand. She leaned into his shoulder, the satin material of her rich, red gown rustling with her movement. Manchester removed the quill from his inside pocket and placed it in his and Maga's entwined hands. He looked out over the crowd and smiled.

"Over a year ago, my bride and I made a promise to a great woman," Manchester said. "We promised to watch over her godson, Riley. In that time, this has become more than a promise to us. It has become a precious and sacred honor. And so today, we write into law that which is already written upon our hearts. With this very same quill Sir Reginald placed on the stone altar those many centuries past... this very same quill which I removed to become your king... this very same quill which myself and Bugbear used to end the Battle of Tamarack... with this quill I and my Queen now adopt Riley Cox, who from hence forth shall be known as Riley Ratcatcher Manchester, Prince of Patchworks and Duke of the Draig

Gwraig." Together Maga and Manchester signed their names as one upon the parchment before them. And when they finished they bent down to embrace their new son.

The crowd erupted into cheers and applause. "Hail Prince Riley!" they called. "Long live the Patchwork Prince!"

Bugbear nudged the twitching and fidgeting Tudmire. "Why don't you relax and enjoy the moment, cousin?"

"I would," he groaned. "But someone's going to have to clean this up when it's all over."

Bugbear laughed and patted Tudmire on the back. "You've done a splendid job once again, dear Tudmire. But I have a little surprise of my own to unveil." Bugbear nodded and motioned to Bixby and Cobblestone.

The Dabblers pulled the rope and dropped the tarp from the large, mysterious object. The crowd gasped as a majestic bronze statue was revealed. Riley looked upon it, his eyes wide and mesmerized. It was an archer, drawing his bow and aiming his arrow towards the heavens... his feathered hat cocked to the side, his long hair cascading across broad and sturdy shoulders. And at the base of the statue in bold gold letters were emblazoned the words: *"His Bogenschiessen was Best."*

"Pfeil..." Riley gasped.

"I told you he wouldn't be forgotten," Bugbear smiled to the prince.

"You did this?" Maga smiled to Bugbear.

The goblin nodded. "The library is named after Mother Twitchett. So, I thought this might be a nice added touch."

Maga fell to her knees and smothered Bugbear with warm and happy kisses. "Thank you, you dear little man," she laughed.

"Oh dear!" Bugbear blurted. "I suppose this means I'm next in line for adoption!"

The crowd exploded with laughter as Maga pulled out of the embrace and playfully squeezed Bugbear's cheeks.

"Okay," Tudmire said, holding up one hand as the other hand secured his trousers.

"Everyone step aside. Time for the family portrait."

The crowd muttered, mumbled, and meandered aside as the photographer readied the camera.

Then suddenly, like a raging river cresting over a levee, a great and miserable roar shattered the scene, echoing from the town gates and filling every inch of air in its rumbling wake.

"Tembo!" Manchester blurted as he rushed towards the gates. Maga, Bugbear, Riley, and Tudmire followed, as did many of the townsfolk and guests.

At the gates the city guards leveled their rifles at the towering patchwork as he lumbered frantic and wounded along the cobbled street.

"Stand down!" Maga ordered. "He is a friend!"

The incredulous guards did as they were ordered, stepping back with trembling hands clutching their guns.

The giant patchwork slowly knelt to the ground, his body bloody and battered with wounds that would have delivered a creature of lesser prowess into the afterlife. He lowered his mighty arms from his bosom, revealing a sacred burden he had been carrying and protecting.

"It's a dragon bride!" Bugbear gasped.

Maga rushed to her sister as Tembo lowered her to the ground. The dragon bride was as tortured and tattered as her protector, yet beyond her physical condition a madness seemed to devour her round, clouded eyes.

"Sehnaa," Maga whispered as she cradled her broken sister in her arms.

"Maga," Sehnaa sobbed weakly.

"Fetch Doc Glenn," Manchester ordered Riley.

The patchwork nodded grimly and bolted through the crowd like a black and white bullet.

"What happened?" Bugbear asked Tembo.

The giant wheezed and sputtered, trying to frame his agony into words. "My friends and I followed the map King Martin gave us," Tembo started. "We found Cron, plying her wicked arts deep in the bowels of the goblin keep. She had gathered more patchworks to her service, including one nearly as large as myself. A savage and soulless thing of horns, claws, and fangs."

"Pawe," Manchester spat.

"We fought long and hard," Tembo continued. "Anna and Yuri fell. And as I fought off their foot soldiers, Cron and her watchdog fled. I pursued them, but cries for help distracted me. In one of the dungeons I found four of the Queen's kin. This was the only one still alive."

Maga sobbed as she held Sehnaa closer. Manchester placed a hand on his wife's shoulder.

Bugbear quietly walked up to Tembo as the crowd parted to allow Doc Glenn to tend the wounded dragon bride. "Tembo," the goblin whispered into the giant's ear, "the deceased dragon brides... were the... brains removed?"

"Yes," the elephant-lion rumbled softly. "How did you know?"

"I didn't know," the goblin shuddered. "I feared."

Maga held her sister's hand and sang soft and tender songs from their childhood as Pope's men gently bore her on a stretcher to Doc Glenn's office. Manchester started to follow, but Bugbear held him back with a tug of his coattails.

"We need to talk," Bugbear said in a low and secretive tone. "I fear this evil deed has deep and tangled roots."

"Why would Cron torture them like that?" Manchester asked as he knelt down beside his advisor. "Wouldn't it make more sense for her to turn them into patchworks? Or kill them outright?"

"She was seeking information," Bugbear answered.

"What kind of information?"

"Hidden knowledge," the goblin said, closing his eyes as though trying to squeeze the realization from his mind. "A deep and subconscious race memory that only the dragon brides would carry." Bugbear's eyes exploded open, wide and round with fear. He grabbed Manchester by the collar and shook him, as though the words he was about to speak would not be sufficiently startling by themselves. "She knows where the Dragon Graveyard is."

Manchester pulled away from Bugbear and staggered to his feet. He shook his head and stammered. "The... the Dragon Graveyard?"

"The last place on this world where the Dragon's held physical form," the goblin answered. "Where they left their mortal bodies when they ascended to become pure spiritual beings." Bugbear turned away from Manchester. "We were fools," he sighed. "The Baymaari never wanted Washington D.C. or the Áes dána Empire. What they want, what they have always wanted since the dawn of time, is the Dragons. The Battle of Washington wasn't the end of the war. It was simply the first shot."

"I fear this evil deed has deep and tangled roots."

Manchester gazed about, his wide and worried eyes taking in the frantic swarm of activities around the gates of Willow Prairie. Rígan, Asherby, and Tudmire washed and tended to Tembo's wounds, as the citizens hurried back to their homes, shuttering their windows and bolting their doors. Pope barked orders to his men, setting up watch schedules and readying cannons and rifles along the outside parameters. And Loomis, Dubbin, and Nigel closed the heavy wooden gates of Willow Prairie, bolting them shut with a huge timber bar.

"We need to get to the Dragon Graveyard before Cron," Manchester insisted, blinking the disturbing images from his sight as he turned to Bugbear.

"No," Bugbear said with a shake of his head. "Ask our new allies in the U.S. Army and Áes dána military to send forces to intercept Cron and Pawe. For we need to stay here in Willow Prairie and prepare." The goblin turned about, his eyes alight with that old mad glimmer Manchester knew all too well. "If the Baymaari are foolish enough to escalate this war, the Noggle Lords must be ready with an answer."

"Noggle *Lords*?" Manchester said with confusion.

Bugbear nodded with a fevered, conflicting mix of sobriety and madness. "Bixby! Cobblestone!" the goblin called out to the Dabblers as he waddled down the street through the rapidly thinning crowds. "Secure a smithy! We have work to do!"

The End